The Double Door

Theodora Keogh

The New Traveller's Companion Series, #112

THE DOUBLE DOOR
THEODORA KEOGH

FIRST PUBLISHED 1950

ISBN: 1-59654-566-6

THE OLYMPIA PRESS.
A DVISION OF DISRUPTIVE PUBLISHING, INC.

1

THE YOUNG MAN with the wheelbarrow turned down Sixty-fifth Street. It was that brief interval between dusk and dark and in the uncertain light things were disproportionate. One could no longer judge distances. The thick dusk seemed to come not only between the eye and its object but between the ear and its reverberation. The young man's wheelbarrow became a thing of magic: it glowed with half a dozen crimson lights as though giant fireflies had settled on it. The young man was wheeling danger signals to an opening that had just been made in the surface of the street. He crossed an avenue, debonair and at ease. His place here was secure, his destination important. He settled the red lanterns carelessly, in case anyone was looking, and accurately, because he was conscientious, and then walked off into the night.

The street, nursing its fresh and gaping wound, was silent.

It was a district of private houses, more and more of a rarity in central New York. Big business hovered; not so far away, the monster shadow of Rockefeller Center was stretching its claws, but here, in Sixty-fifth Street the skies were as yet unpierced.

In No. 7 only one window was lit up, like a dirty yellow eye, at the very top. No. 5, however, was clear-eyed; the light from there streamed out into the street in white rectangles. There would really have been no need for the little red lanterns. No. 5 and No. 7, side by side, touching shoulder and flank, looked as different as could be: born at different times, one would have sworn, and from different parents. Yet they were joined. An artery as heavy and brutal as that which binds Siamese twins ran through them both. Their bloods met in it and fought and were sickened. This artery, this freak passageway, was through the Duke Charles de

Tudelos' bedroom. Here there was a double door which he often used and which other people used too. The Duke found it quite natural that two houses should belong to him. He was immensely rich, or rather his wife was. If he needed two houses to express his personality, he had the right to own them.

At this instant he was coming through from No. 7 to No. 5. The double door was always open. Sometimes, especially of late, his wife Sheila would stand there for minutes on end, looking down the dark old-fashioned halls of her husband's other home. She would not go in, however. He could count on that. He half expected to find her there now, near the double door, and was preparing a scene. After all, they had guests downstairs and someone should be there. Guests were such pigs, one could never trust them hostless for long! Charles was tired. He loosened the sash of his robe and sat on his bed. The lids of his large eyes drooped and twitched. He hesitated between a purge and a benzedrine tablet: perhaps the benzedrine tablet now, and the purge before he went to bed. He sighed. Things were getting out of control again, and, after all, it was his wife's money. People had no consideration! Charles de Tudelos often wondered what he would have done had Sheila not fallen in love with him. Would he have been happier? Freer, certainly; less plagued by a conception of life which was not his own and which split his actions and his thoughts in two. He switched on the phonograph—part of his built-in set—and put a needle on the disc that was already there. A voice came out: *"Si mes vers avaient des ailes..."* *If my verses had wings.* How tender and womanly that little song sounded in New York! In Paris it was an ordinary dime-a-dozen song, but here it brought back all the sad, sweet thrill of love that is not quite reciprocated. A young girl, one might fancy, sacrificing herself, effacing herself, for love of an important man—a general or a great artist. She only asks that he take his pleasure of her, and his comfort, while she stays in obscurity, singing melodiously at a darkening window.

The only person who had ever loved him, Charles, that way was Sheila, and it was she who had been important then rather than he. It was to him that she had come with all her father's wealth. To him: the nobody, the go-between, the gigolo. Beneath his silk robe Charles' feet tapped uncomfortably at the memory. He had on black, pointed shoes, and no one save himself could tell the difference between the left and the right. He supposed he should interchange them to make them last longer, but he was so used to the slight difference caused by use that it would be uncomfortable. Maybe the next time he had them resoled—The cobbler, there was a brawny fellow! With this reflection he stood up and took off his robe, turning away from the mirror so as not to see his narrow chest, his thin, flabby upper arm. The skin was gathered and ocher in the indentations of his body. Diet and purge had failed to eliminate the paunch that hung from his waist. He quickly put on a white shirt, and as he did so, heard someone going down the stairs of No. 7, past his open door and on down to the street. He did not turn his head. The little room upstairs in No. 7 would, he knew, now be dark over the dark street.

"Charles, are you coming down soon?"

He turned quickly to where the voice came from. Sheila, his wife, stood in the study just beyond his room; to the good side, that was, well into No. 5.

"Comme tu es ennuieuse!" he cried. "How you torment me! Can't you stay quiet for an hour without coming to make me scenes?" He spoke in a high, nasal voice which shot up from his lungs to ricochet down through his long, curved nose. Although nothing his wife had actually said justified his harsh and irritated reply, yet he was certain she was coming to quarrel, and his certainty was rewarded when Sheila burst immediately into tears.

Sheila was a big woman with long, thin legs and a full body. She had a hennaed friz about her face, and this face was also long and terribly pale. Tears (of all varieties) had literally worn furrows in her cheeks and almost extinguished the original twinkle of her small eyes.

"They're *your* guests," she shrilled. "All of them. Not one is *my* friend."

As if to make him manly despite himself, as a revenge or a punishment, Sheila's voice was glued to the roof of her head. It was like the piping of a petulant and sickly bird. Charles was sure she did it on purpose. No matter how high a note he reached in affectation and rage, that sickly little bird-bitch outflew him easily.

He stamped his pointed foot as he answered her: "Why do you say that? You are constantly insinuating things. If you want to ask anyone to our house all you have to do is to pick up the phone or give an order to the secretary."

"But I wouldn't like to have my friends here with that awful mob. You insult them yourself."

"How dare you speak that way of some of the greatest society of New York and Europe!" He was working himself up and could probably be heard by the guests themselves.

She came a step further towards his room and said in her precise accent: "Why do you agree not to let Candy go down there if you think of them so highly?"

At these words the husband and wife looked surprised, stopped in their tracks, and took time to reflect. Charles, still without trousers, wondered if his legs appeared ridiculous below his white shirt tails and if the large vein below his ear were not overswollen. It throbbed. Sheila concentrated on gazing at the bedside lamp. By half shutting her swimming eyes, she made a rainbow and the exercise made her feel childish and protected.

Neither thought of Candy, because Candy was too troubling for serious thought. One could bully and instruct, one could even kiss and admire, but one could not, one dare not, think deeply of Candy.

"Well, if you go away, *cherie,* and let me dress I'll come down."

"Oh, it's all right," she said. "I'm going to my room now anyway."

She turned and wandered off aimlessly with her awkward, toed-in gait. Her thin feet, her long, calfless legs appeared touching and girlish. Beneath the hopeless maturity of her body they had remained frail and young. The sight of them made Charles uneasy, they were an indication of what he feared. Suppose his wife in one of her clumsy, immature moments were to say something so direct that he would have to understand her? In a way, the idea of such a thing thrilled as much as it horrified him.

He put on his trousers and brushed his hair—it was dyed black—into a lifeless sheen. He powdered his face carefully, and to no effect, since the shadow sprang out again on cheek and jaw. Taking a hairpin, he dipped it into the contents of a jar and ran it along the inside of his eyelids. It was kohl that he used. Next he took out his handkerchief and sprinkled it with an extremely musky perfume. By this time the benzedrine had taken effect and he felt much better. A kind of exaltation had replaced his lassitude. Now he could go among his guests. He hurried down the stairs, making inarticulate cries of greeting.

The Duquesa, who had not closed the door of her room, heard the patter of his feet on the stairs and his greetings to the crowd that thronged their house almost every day. It was true that none of them were friends of hers and that in her heart she at once envied and despised them all. She was too worldly not to know why they came and too innocent to derive any satisfaction from the power of her tremendous wealth. *Life* was what she wanted: a close, ardent, simple life, such a one as she would never have.

She walked back again into Charles' study and wandered idly about the room, trailing her hands over desk and chair. From the two big windows she could look out on the street and see the light from the floor below reflected on the broken slabs of tarred paving. Her mind, as she wandered back and forth, felt heavy and dense. What a terrible burden love was and how bitterly long it lasted! Charles, of course, had never loved her at all, and every day she made him ugly scenes so that by nightfall the collection and rehearsal of them added fresh weight to her leaden brain. When she thought about her life, there were only three days of it that were sweet, and they were long past. To recall them was a necessity for Sheila; to replace each incident, each word and gesture. There had been, besides and to begin with, a kiss: the only one she had received from a man in her whole life that was neither forced nor dutiful. Lately, even this kiss was marred in her memory by doubt.

Sheila was crying again now, and from both her long cheeks the powder was quite gone, leaving her brow and chin unnaturally white. Her tears were not really those of grief but simply of habit. She began talking aloud to herself, softly yet vehemently, punctuating her thought: "No, no— I'll show him—Tomorrow I'll be different—Surely I will, I will—" She repeated these phrases again and again; tomorrow, by some miracle, she would be so perfect that her husband would fall at her feet in adoration.

Sheila was a monster and Charles often told her so.

The six red lanterns in the street began to attract her notice as she tired of her emotion. They winked in the frosty air. She pressed her face against the cold windowpane and stared out at the danger signals while an idea took possession of her. It was one of those ideas or impulses that come to girls and women during periods of change. She went quickly into her own room and started opening and shutting drawers. Being accustomed to having someone else put all her things in order, she did not know where to look.

Finally she gave up and stood helplessly in the center of the jumble she had made: drawers half out, closets ajar, hats thrown on bed and chair. The solution occurred to her as she was returning to the study. Of course, her brooch! It was the very thing, and made of gold, which added to her mental picture. As she removed it, the stuff of her dress caught and she jerked at the pin angrily until it came free with some velvet threads still attached. Sheila decided to perform her rite while sitting at the desk which the secretary used during the day. From her seat there she could just see the street. She looked at it steadily as she pushed up the sleeve from her left arm and jabbed the pin into the intense white of her skin. She gave a little cry. The pain astonished her. She had not expected to feel anything and was indignant at doing so.

At that moment someone coming from the other house walked through the Duke's room and appeared timidly at the threshold of the study. It was a monk dressed in a white robe, with a book in his hand.

"Ah, good evening, Pere Laborde." Sheila gave him a glance full of disdain. She knew he hated her presence here because it morally obstructed the freedom of his passage from one house to the other.

He noticed her rolled-back sleeve and the heavy drop of blood on her arm. "Good evening," he returned. "Have you hurt yourself?"

Sheila got the impression of his physical recoil, not at her slight wound but at the thought, the obscure, feminine impulse, behind it. "I was going to make six," she answered spitefully, and looked out again at the street, "but it hurts too much after all."

2

** Candy's diary:*

.......My name is Maria Tudelos and I am called Candy *de* Tudelos. It seems when I was at that stage of infancy where one is a genius, the word *candy* was forever on my lips, and at about that time Papa bought his title, which explains both changes. Yesterday was my fifteenth birthday and Pere Laborde gave me this diary, with a little speech about the pure and sacred thoughts of a young girl. I want to use the first few pages to explain what I am. (Why? Do I want anyone to read this? How vulgar!)

First, my looks. I am rather tall for my age, with thin legs, thank God (or thank Mama). Two months ago I thought I was getting fat but I dieted. Aside from this I appear to be the perfect jeune fille bien elevee—rather old-fashioned. A long tail of black hair swinging against my spine, drawn back from a scrubbed face. I wear blouses or sweaters and brown, shined oxfords with beige socks. All very well but don't be deceived (dear reader?), there are other aspects. Let me turn my head just a little, not too much, as my profile is pure cameo, but just a little—so—There! Don't you see that flattish, wooden look? That almost stupid look? And my eyes, they *are* narrow, aren't they?

Papa thinks that by keeping me quiet and studious and not letting me have friends he can drive the Indian (there, the word is out!) blood from my veins. Does he think he has done so already? Oh how he would love to be the noble Spaniard he pretends! Alas! He never went to Spain at all until after he was married. He comes instead from some small country in South America which it is my affectation not to know the name of. How ashamed he is of that. I am not ashamed. I am ashamed of nothing. I was born without shame.

To go on with the fascinating subject of my looks, my nose is straight and about the same thickness all the way, as though a white line had been drawn down the bridge as actresses do. My lashes, upper and lower, are black, shiny and long and my skin is clear, aside from a few freckles which I inherited from Mama along with my legs and which hardly ever show. Shall I escape spots altogether or will they come later? My mouth is small, what the French call spirituelle, with curved lips, curved on the inside, that is. The line starts deep at the corners and forms a little beak in the center, like the lips of old statues, only not as thick—What else? Oh yes, I have nice hands. Along my arms and wrists I have—not down, dear reader—but hairs. They are like straight black threads. Are you shocked? Do I like them? I think I do. They are the finest and thinnest of black lines and the skin between them looks very white.

In my role of jeune fille bien elevee I have as yet no figure, so I will leave that to your imagination, especially as I know Pere Laborde will try and read this on the sly and a priest should know nothing about women. (Don't worry, *mon Pere,* I am sure you are spotless in that respect.)

Now I shall reluctantly pass on to my character. In what part of me is my soul? In what part of me is my heart? This is my biggest secret and it is extraordinary that I have known it as far back as I can remember, since I was two and a half years old, to be exact. Poor Mother carries her heart in her bosom and her soul on her cheeks, where it is continually bathed in tears. As for Papa, he can never find his at the right moment and there is always a great search going on, and then, when he finally gets hold of something, like as not it is the wrong one for the occasion. I find that those observations arc quite clever but perhaps I read them somewhere—Oh, I was going to tell you where *I* kept things. In my head. They fit in neatly and can be controlled by my mind, which is clear at all times.

The next question is who does Candy love in the world?

The answer to that is a blank. I know nothing at all of the subject and have never seen any evidences of it around me.

To pass on—what interests Candy de Tudelos?

***

As Candy wrote these words she stopped and put the pointed end of her penholder between her teeth. They, the teeth, still had bands with elastics on either side, but she had said nothing about them in her description. To her mind's eye they had been removed long ago. What *did* interest Candy de Tudelos? Her inner eye traveled over the surface of her quiet, studious, child's life: the lessons with Pere Laborde, the books she got from The Society Library, the walks with her maid Josie; and the early supper she took upstairs in her own room at night. The supper, she thought, represented her life the best: an omelette, a salad, a little fruit. No, it was not in these things her interest lay and she could find no others. Was she simply biding her time? That must be it. The moment would come, it had to, when she would feel between her fingers the veritable stuff, the pure silk, of existence.

Candy thought a few minutes more and then wrote another sentence in her diary. After her last question—What interests Candy de Tudelos?—she put the words: No. 7. Then she closed the book, which was made of a beautiful, pink pigskin. The edges of the thick pages were gold, and she now locked it with a little gold key. 'Where shall I hide my key?' she mused, and wondered further: 'Just how difficult do I wish to make the search?'

Candy was forever asking herself questions, not in anguish or soul-searching, as is sometimes the case with adolescents, but clearly, out of her clear, crystal heart whose place she thought to know so well. She got up, smoothing her skirt and walked to the bureau. The stately, almost arrogant quality of her walk was mixed with the awkwardness of extreme youth and lack of sufficient muscular training. The result was baffling.

At this moment Josie, maid, governess and duenna, came nervously into the room.

"Ah Josie, where shall I hide the key to my diary?"

"Why Miss Candy, you may hide it wherever you like, I am sure no one would read anything of yours without asking. It would certainly be dishonest." Josie blinked her eyes rapidly behind thick, distorting lenses.

"Do I detect irony, my dear Josie? Denying a thing does not help. Besides, I *expect* people to pry. Of course I don't mean you! I want the *right* people to be able, after a long, humiliating search, to find the key and read all about themselves. Can't you see them, fumbling and hasty, horrified at such a good picture of all they thought I didn't notice?"

"Miss Candy, how foolish you are today!" Josie was blushing, which she did unevenly, and looking furtively towards the door. She was afraid of being overheard.

"But Josie, *try* to see it. They'd be blushing just as you are now, just as badly, but from rage. And then, just as they got to the worst bit, I'd come in and there they'd be!" Candy came up to the older woman and took her rough hand. "Don't be so nervous, darling Josie. What if anyone *should* come in now, this very moment? *You* are doing nothing but scolding me, a very virtuous occupation, the perfect thing to be caught doing. Anyway, I am not talking of anyone in particular. You, Josie, are my only friend in this whole house—or in the other, either." Still clasping that rough, calloused hand, Candy put her face very near the servant's and tried to look in her eyes. She repeated softly: "Or in the other house either. Isn't that so?"

Josie's eyes, enlarged behind their lenses, could be seen sliding and shifting. She could not meet the young girl's gaze. The smooth, cool beauty of that face so close to hers hurt her, made her wish to cry. How young those features were and, as a whole, how utterly youthless! 'She should be playing with children her own age, going to school like everyone else. It's a stupid crime and *they* can only pay for it in the end,' thought Josie. She said aloud: "Miss Candy, the best friend of every man or woman is the one that bore them."

"How sweet! Why couldn't I think of that myself? Rather risque though, don't you think? All mixed up with conceiving, which I'm not supposed to know about."

"Which you *don't* know about and which I shan't talk about, and if you don't behave I shan't ask you to walk to Fifty-first Street as I had planned. Your mother suggested I take you as that piano teacher isn't to be here any more."

Candy turned away carelessly. Josie was not deceived. The child had paled. She was not one to whine or stammer, but she sometimes showed her hand by the pallor which extinguished the color of her cheeks and lips. Now a few freckles above her eyebrows could be seen quite plainly. Poor Candy! Her life, with its sparse interest, was continually being cut out from under her. Just as an occupation took hold and its teacher gained her attention, some strong, passionate blast would blow them out of the house, teacher and occupation both, out of her life. Now she dropped the key in a drawer and said casually:

"Very well, Josie, I'll just put on my coat."

They went out a few minutes later. The day was cold and there were patches of ice on the streets from old—now that had melted and frozen. There was a wind, too, which blew great eddies of dust in their faces.

"Josie," cried Candy, "smell the sewers!" She made a grimace. "I suppose we shall have that smell the rest of the winter."

As Candy spoke, one of the workmen came up, putting on his jacket. He wrenched at the sleeves to force his muscular arms all the way in. He was a stocky young fellow with black curly hair, the workman who nightly set up the red lanterns on the street. Overhearing the girl's remark, he looked at her an instant as he drew abreast. His face was brown but not ruddy. The drops of sweat still clinging to brow and upper lip gave him that touching air of virility that is the beauty of young, simple men. Candy's eyes were on exactly the same level as his. She was on the sidewalk, while he was still in the street, and so their glances locked. His eyes also were fringed with thick, black lashes, but they were more open than hers; large, liquid, Italian orbs fixed on Candy.

"Hey, Giovanni! Hurry up! We ain't got all day." It was another workman's voice and the young man blinked. His stare was broken and he passed on hurriedly to where his companion waited.

"Keep your shirt on, Mike," he called loudly. "I'm coming as fast as I can." His voice sounded thick. His words were reformed in a white mist in front of his face.

Candy, who had been walking arm in arm with Josie, drew away abruptly, making Josie drop her purse.

"Miss Candy! Whatever is the matter with you today? Do you know what I think?"—She was about to say that it was time Candy went to parties or else to boarding school, but she restrained herself. After all these years she would have been a fool if she had not at least learned how to hold her tongue. Aside from Harris the butler, she was the oldest retainer in the Tudelos household, and the reason was that she was ugly, had looked old since the age of twenty-five, and never stood up for herself or anyone else.

Candy, however, did not hear the question. She walked skittishly on the icy street and clenched her hands in their peccary gloves. The bitter wind that flicked dust and specks of coal against her face felt warm on her cheeks. Such a rush of warmth mounted in her veins that she was half stifled. She opened the collar of her brown, belted coat and let the wind blow in on her neck and the top part of her breast. The skin there grew mottled, chafed by the unaccustomed cold, but she felt nothing. Could she have bared her whole breast, she would have done so.

"Josie," she cried, "how slow you are! I am so happy, Josie! Josie, is it nicer to be young or old?" She leaned her head from side to side so that the air would reach and cool the throbbing lobes of her ears.

The servant answered her: "They say youth is the only thing worth having in the world, Miss Candy. I wouldn't know. I never had pleasure when I was young and I can't say being old is much better. But there you are, I'm only a poor woman. It is the rich who can enjoy life." Josie spoke this last in a jargon false and set with repetition and use. These, for some reason, were the sentiments expected of such as she. Far from offending, they gave satisfaction, bringing a secret, triumphant smile to the lips of her employers.

Candy, however, stopped prancing and said sharply: "How stupid you are, Josie. Stupid and false. I told you you were my only friend and I ask you a simple question. Why do you give me the same act you would give to Mama? Why are you so insipid?"

"Call it what you like, it's the truth." Josie went back on her dignity.

Candy laughed. "Mother and Father are so rich and they're deliriously happy, aren't they? It's touching to see two people so united, so in love."

"Miss Candy, a joke's a joke, but you must not speak ill of your parents before me. It isn't proper."

"Speak ill? Why I was only saying nice things. I was talking about love, and do you know why? Do you? I'll tell you why, since you keep on mincing primly along with your mouth closed. I'll just tell you anyway. Because I'm in love! That's why—there!"

"In love!" Josie was utterly surprised. "In love with whom?"

Candy took hold of Josie's arm once again and said nothing for a few moments. Then, hugging the poor, scrawny, sinewy arm against her own, she cried: "I am in love with *you,* Josie. Your banality has captured my heart. The beauty of your prominent bones has enthralled my senses. *Will* you marry me?"

3

CANDY WAS IN no hurry to get to her afternoon lesson and once past the double door she stood at the stair-head in No. 7, listening to the sounds that are in all old houses. Her hand, small and well shaped, lay on the banister and in this hand Candy betrayed a certain timid girlishness. Even in the dim, motey hall her profile shone; her nose triumphed over youth by the straight bone within, and the fold of her lips was arrogantly quiet. Down in his room on the ground floor she could hear Pere Laborde stirring. Candy always thought of him as 'the priest,' even while calling him *mon Pere.* Picturing him moving around his room in his whitish, ill-smelling robes, she drew her upper lip into an arc of disgust.

There was a sound below and the front door to No. 7 opened. From where Candy was standing, she could see a man's figure outlined against the afternoon light. The man entered, drawing his latchkey awkwardly out of the door, tugging and twisting at the old-fashioned lock before he could get it free.

"Papa must have just given it to him," noted Candy, the observant.

The man closed the door and looked around him with a belligerent twist of his shoulders. Then he started up the stairs and it was not until they were almost touching that Candy recognized Giovanni—Giovanni, the young workman whose eyes had met hers in the street. Here, in the perpetual twilight of No. 7, they passed each other again, for the second time, with no word spoken. Candy stood coolly aside to let the stranger go by and felt on her cheek his harsh, angry, male breath as he stomped up the last step. He turned the corner, walked down the hall, ignoring the double door (perhaps he did not yet know of its existence), and climbed up the second flight of stairs. She heard his feet doggedly alternating above her, and her hand on the banister trembled slightly. Then she skimmed down with her mixture of awkwardness and pride, to knock at the priest's door.

"Mon Pere," she called softly. At once the door opened and the Dominican stood there with his head slightly bent to the side in an effort at whimsicality. He was thin and of medium height, with hardly any cartilage to his nose. His face, because of this, had a medieval, mortal look and he could be pleased to know that here was a contour less frail than flesh. The nostrils, unguarded, burrowed black and hairless into his face. His upper lip was long and his mouth spinsterish. Under his arms the white stuff of his dress was horribly rank. The acid sweat had eaten into the cloth, changing its color and quality. He was in love with Candy, so intensely that it made him feel faint when she approached, yet even had he not been under vow he could never have joined himself to a woman. His love grew because it was so safe, so impossible. Besides, he knew he

revolted her and often took a sort of bitter delight in the fact. He told himself that she was so pure, so utterly virginal, that any near approach of man would repulse her instinctively. Sometimes he purposely tried to aggravate this repulsion.

Today, seeing her so serene and fresh, with her smooth hair and schoolgirl's blouse, he could not help making a violent gesture with his arm so that the stench of his armpit struck her like a blow in the face. Candy recoiled visibly, narrowing her eyes and opening her mouth a little. She could never make up her mind whether on such occasions it was better to breathe through the mouth or the nose. If the former, one smelt nothing, but on the other hand, one was less protected. The poison could go down unsifted into one's lungs.

Candy turned aside and went into another room where there was a ping-pong table and two grey windows looking out curtainless onto a grey yard. It was here she took her lessons. Pere Laborde followed his pupil with the books. They sat side by side. First they read a chapter of French history, and Candy managed, while listening dutifully, to give the impression that his voice was monotonous. Pere Laborde finished reading and opened an algebra textbook with secret reluctance. They were soon due to reach the point where his knowledge or memory stopped. Candy, who was bright, could have strained maliciously, but she got more pleasure out of watching and waiting. Already he must check her answers from a master text, and she contented herself with flicking her eyes his way as he did so. Sometimes he would try to hide his subterfuge behind his hand, pretending at the same time to do the problem aloud. Her glance then stung him like a nettle.

Their last subject was Literature and they were finishing *Hamlet.* Pere Laborde adored the play because the principal character had possibilities, from his point of view. The idea of the black prince, with his complicated feelings, his private torments, was soothing and could be turned in many ways.

"Hamlet's mother wasn't really committing incest, *mon Pere,"* said Candy. "I don't understand all the disturbance he makes."

The priest resented her probing. She should leave the meanings of such things alone. They were secret signs, he felt, for him and his like—milestones at which to rest and draw breath. He leaned close to his pupil and Candy could look down the dark tunnels of his face and feel her own cheeks polluted by his breath. She drew back slightly and tried to look elsewhere.

The room was large and dusk had come to the dirty windows, pressing against them with the chill wind. The ping-pong table was too high and its edges cut at her breasts. Something in the thick dimming of light and in the quality of the air made her recall another day three years ago when, as a skinny black-haired child with bare knees, she had skipped through the double door one afternoon. She had wanted to elude Josie and be alone a little while. Pere Laborde was already intermittently her tutor, but at that particular time he had been away, either in France or Canada. In the ping-pong room three youths had been playing, and Candy had trotted down the stairs, invisible in the darkness of the hall.

"Say, let's go into the old monk's room and see what we can find!"

They had thrown down their rackets at this suggestion—three good-looking young men with thick unruly hair. They had giggled nervously as they rummaged among another person's things. Candy could see them through the open door, pulling out one of the long white robes from the closet and opening bureau drawers.

"Come here, Greg, look at this!"

There had been exclamations of delight. Candy had moved along the hall silently in order to be in on the discovery. In among the white linen underthings they had come upon a tube of lipstick and a box of mascara. The boy called Greg had seized the lipstick and, forcing it to its full length, had applied it to his lips, looking the while in the dresser mirror. He had smoothed the brilliant paste tenderly with his little finger until his mouth was completely covered and the other boys had looked on. They were intent now and the atmosphere was charged.

"Oh!" cried one, "God! Doesn't it make you—" He took Greg's shoulders and shook them. "I'm so angry, so *mad!"*

Candy had been able to make nothing of this, flattened against the wall in the dark. It was just more senseless grownup talk. But then all three had seemed to come alive and get excited. They painted absurdly curved lips on each other and blackened each other's lashes. One put on the monk's white robe and another undid his plaid shirt, pulling it apart, and rouged the bones between his flat breasts. They minced around and lit cigarettes until Candy had to put both hands in front of her face to stop herself laughing.

The late afternoon light paled their skins on which the makeup stood out in relief.

All of a sudden Candy had found her feelings changed. It was not so funny anymore. The three boys, once so handsome and gay, looked eaten now by some frightful plague. It was as though their faces, the cheeks and lips, were devoured by live sores, by polluted blood crawling beneath the skin. Their black lashes had smeared and circled their lids with the exhaustion of disease. And, as in old paintings, drawn and colored in the Dark Ages, they flaunted their sores and relished them.

Then, one by one, they had begun to dance. They stripped to the waist and postured around the room, with long pauses in front of the mirror. They thrust out their hips and arched their backs. Greg took off his belt and started hitting the others. Candy had heard the leather slap hard against bare skin but no one had acted hurt. They had completely stopped talking. She had heard the rasp of their breath as they exerted and twisted their bodies.

And was it the child in the hall three years ago who saw Giovanni enter and take his place among them? No, of course not. Giovanni was not around in those days. Yet the fifteen-year-old Candy, sitting now beside Pere Laborde, saw him clearly. Surely, he had entered. He had swaggered among them in workclothes, with the beads of sweat still on his face. He had looked around him, and then, as though he too were drawn by the same compulsion, had undone his shirt and let it hang from his belt with the sleeves falling to his calves. His breast was crossed with black hair. His teats were like gold coins. He picked up the rouge from the bureau, but it was getting so dark that Candy could not tell the expression on his face. She tried to call out:

"Giovanni, Giovanni! Don't do that! There *must* be another way." But after all, a twelve-year-old child is mute, crouched in a hallway where it has no business to be. The fifteen-year-old Candy, however, made a little involuntary sound.

"What is the matter, *ma chere,* are you unwell?" The priest laid his hand on her arm.

"Quite well, *mon Pere,"* Candy replied, putting a touch of surprise into her voice.

Something in her tone brought Pere Laborde up sharply. Could Candy be intimating that he had asked an indelicate question? Was she that perverse? He did not dare look at her, and inside him some devil's yeast started to ferment. The thought that he might at this moment be sitting next to such a terrible, such a mysterious phenomenon, clouded his brain and made the hand on her arm tighten convulsively.

Candy shrugged her arm away. "By the way, *mon Pere,* you should be more careful to lock your door when you go on tour. People can go in."

"Have *you* ever done so?" He made an effort to recover himself and to sound light.

"What possible reason could *I* have?"

"Oh, curiosity; to find out how one of us mysterious priests lives."

"Curiosity? Do you have secrets, *mon Pere?"*

"None other than chastity, poverty, and Godliness, my child, I'm afraid."

At that, Candy looked at him in such a way that he wished he could think of a gesture more brutal than usual, but he could not. Candy turned her face slightly away from him, and he could see the blind, animal head—wooden, impassive, Indian.

4

GIOVANNI PUCHINI WAS not a remarkable young man. In many ways he was stupid. He was not even very sensitive or very imaginative. He was, however, Italian, and that can make up for a lot. Who is whiter of tooth, more black and curly of hair, more easy of speech than an Italian? If he is obvious, it is only the more winning. And they know their charm, a grace in itself.

Giovanni had grown up by the East River and had been born in New York. Before that event took place the Puchini family lived in Rome, on a mean little island in the Tiber. The swift brown water flowed on either side, and from her window Giovanni's mother could see the huge Cloaca Maxima vomiting into the river day and night. Nearby a broken bridge of extraordinary beauty plunged its limbs into the filthy flood. Towards evening, rats as bold as dogs roved the neighborhood, their teeth gleaming, the antique plague in their pelts. For none of these things did Mrs. Puchini's heart beat the faster. She was much too busy having children, being milked by them and gaining weight. At night her husband came home, singing and half full of wine, to grab his mate playfully by the folds of her flesh, and she conceived Giovanni just as they were planning to leave for America. The idea of changing countries had come from Mrs. Puchini's sister who had gone over as a girl. The sister kept writing and describing the manifold wonders of the New World, until finally there was nothing left for them to do but migrate.

All this had been almost nineteen years ago and they had left off having children with Giovanni. Mr. Puchini had become an iceman, and when Giovanni was eleven years old his aunt had been strangled to death in her little whore's bedroom in the West Fifties. It had had no frightening effect on the boy, although he could recall his mother's shrieks and the excitement and pride of the event. In those days he had been very busy playing by the river, fighting other river gangs, and worshiping a fiery-headed Irish mick who was their leader.

Things had seemed nice in those days, and while Giovanni, the grown-up workingman of eighteen, was swinging away with his pick or holding the great drill which made his bones tremble, he often wished for the return of the old, lazy life. Giovanni, however, was a good boy and brought home most of his pay to his two-hundred-pound mother, whom he loved. They had a railroad flat on Second Avenue, and now that all his sisters and brothers were married, Giovanni even slept in a room all alone.

Mrs. Puchini was usually in the kitchen when her son got home from work. He would come up and kiss her steamy, congested cheek before doing anything else, often interrupting a song to do it, just like his father. Tonight he did not sing. Instead of looking in on his mother, he went straight to his room and closed the door. Then he stretched out on the bed with his arms under his head and stared up at the ceiling.

'A week ago,' he thought, 'I was hardly any younger. Ma was in the kitchen just like she is now. I was working under Regan too, just like today, horsing around with Mike and all.' He went on telling himself the things that had been the same then as now, wrinkling his tawny forehead and hitting the toes of his boots together. As he went on down the list a lump seemed to grow in the pit of his stomach, and when he got to the end and could not think of anything else, it was a stone wound in his entrails. There he was, looking straight at those clear eyes, windows into a dark room. He could trace their long outline in his mind and see the black, separated lashes.

And this was painful and the rock moved in his entrails, for Giovanni was in love with Candy. He had seen her only twice—once in the street and once on the stairway of No. 7, but even had he seen her once and never again, it would have made no difference. Perhaps he was one of those examples of love at first sight in which many people do not believe. Candy was to him like a lightning flash or a clap of thunder. Her first glance was lightning in his veins, and as she passed, the rhythm of his heart was like thunder. He did not think of her as his, or in bed or naked, and he planned nothing, but there was to be only one love for Giovanni in all his life and it was Candy. No matter how long he lived, or whom he slept with or conceived by, it would never come again. Something had shifted within him, not in his brain exactly, nor in his heart or senses, but rather in those stubborn recesses of a man where a shift is final, because none can reach in to set things back in place.

So Giovanni lay there, with the strong, round muscles of his upper arm pillowing his head, and felt the ache of love and the weight of it inside his body.

Other things, too, had been happening to him in the last couple of days of which he ought to be thinking, yet he could not seem to attach any importance to them. Even when he drew his arm away from its position and held the wrist up in front of him to look at what was on it, it made no impression. He heard his father come in, jovial and loud, and a resounding slap on his mother's bottom. He blinked his eyes with their girlish fringe and stretched. Then he got up and went into the kitchen.

Giovanni's mother noticed the wrist watch right away.

"Where did you get that?" she asked in Italian.

He answered in English: "Man gave it to me for pay."

"Pay for what, Giovanni?"

"Some work I did for him. Say, do you *have* to talk Italian? Can't you speak English like a human being?"

By now they could hardly be heard. Mr. Puchini, with the native Italian's love of noise for its own sake, was singing and shouting as he poured wine into his glass. The wine was in a gallon jug and he held it over his shoulder to balance the weight.

Giovanni's mother did not believe her son about the watch. She thought a woman had given it to him—possibly a widow who had inherited it and liked the taste of youth on her mouth. Mrs. Puchini was not disturbed by the possibility; there was something else eating her reflections, chewing the cud of her spare thoughts softly, one by one.

In most people's lives there is some drama being played, although if it happens slowly it is hardly realized. For this Mediterranean woman the curtain was well up. She was beginning to be ensnared, even obsessed. To put it plainly, she had fallen into the hands of a sorcerer.

About two weeks ago Mrs. Puchini had gone to Saint Patrick's Cathedral to light a candle for one of her daughters' fourth confinement. Afterwards she had stood on the steps for a moment and looked across over Fifth Avenue at the unknown territory of Rockefeller Center. Not a woman to notice things, as a rule, today the cold blue air settling down around those granite slabs touched some part of her memory. In front of her eyes the buildings appeared endowed with a new order, or rather they were clothed with an old vision. All she had hoped to find in America, all her dreams, gathered themselves together again and she left Fifth Avenue to find herself walking among those white cliffs with a nostalgia she had not experienced heretofore. It was as though her own youth were thus revisited; every aspiration of her young wifehood was symbolized in the clean stone, the square corners, the large, even windows. All was modern and light, no place for vermin. Even the dusk lingered, and the young couples strolling hand in hand were like herself with the lover she should have had long ago: the lover all women should have had, and whose mask the husband wears so deceitfully, discards so soon.

A sharp pain in her bosom had brought Mrs. Puchini out of her reflections. Someday she would go to the clinic about it, but she was afraid of American doctors. They were all for opening you up and discussing you as though you were a rag doll. She preferred something more personal. Besides, here, although they had strong medicine, they had terrible diseases for which there was no cure. In Italy there was always a cure. If all else failed, there were relics and pilgrimages. Suppose, for instance, she had a cancer? Trapped in this land, she would surely die. Once the doctors knew about it, that is. If she never went to the clinic they would never discover it and she might perhaps escape. A narrow chill went down the red, thick column of her neck. She felt the winter wind as it swept around Fifty-second Street from Central Park. It blew coal dust up in swirls from the sidewalk and a black particle lodged in her eye. She was bewildered, buffeted and miserable, and could no longer see in which direction she was going since the tears were pouring down her cheeks. So it was that Mrs. Puchini met her fate.

Rockefeller Plaza is a small cross-street two blocks long. Those who wish to get from one side to the other may take a choice of crossing it or going underground in the tunnels of Rockefeller Center, by which it is bounded east and west. On that day a little fair had been set up in this street. A yellow and red carrousel for very young children was being dismantled for the night and someone had thrown a dark green piece of canvas over the Punch and Judy show with its terrible menage. At the door of his tent the fortuneteller, a man, was stooping to come out when Mrs. Puchini passed with tears running out of her left eye and skirts blowing above her knees.

"Madam," he said, "may I offer you shelter?" And he had put his gloved hand under her elbow.

Inside the tent it was black as pitch and Mrs. Puchini felt confused and ashamed. The cold darkness shut out the sounds of the city, while beside her an unknown man breathed. He had struck a match and lit an oil lantern, red like those which border street constructions and which her son must even now be lighting in the Sixties. Its glow crimsoned the triangle of cloth which sheltered them and she saw a low table with a stool on either side.

"If you will be seated, Madam, you will hear what is in your cards."

Mrs. Puchini in her embarrassment grew coquettish. "Oh my, an old, fat woman like me! What can they say?" She fumbled at her disheveled hair and, misjudging the distance, fell heavily onto the stool. She was completely flustered. The man had the quality of making her self-conscious. She could feel her weight, her body, as she had never done before.

Then, as he leaned across the table, she had seen a pack of cards in his hand. Her eyes flew up and away from that magic pack and, too shy to look at his face, were arrested by his thick white hair. In the lantern's glow it had had a rosy tinge which was somehow sinister.

"What if there is danger for you ahead?" he had asked in his rather metallic voice. "Forewarned is sometimes saved."

"Danger! You make-a-me scared. Who would want to hurt an old woman like-a-me?" She used again the word "old" because it was reassuring but the word "fat" she avoided. Beneath her rusty black coat and alpaca dress her thighs were moist as she tried to hold them together. No matter how she squeezed, the flesh prevented her knees from closing, and the stool was ridiculously small for her. She had been ashamed and humiliated, almost afraid. He answered her:

"Some dangers come from within."

Mrs. Puchini's heart gave a leap. Like a dog who receives a kick, it jumped and was cowed inside her chest. She said eagerly and humbly: "What do they say, Mister?"

He began setting out the cards. They were not like any she had seen before and she had become convinced that whatever they told her would be true for evermore.

So it had begun, and Mrs. Puchini could not see its end. For this she went about her housework with an abstracted expression and saw her husband and son with half an eye only.

Giovanni now went to the kitchen sink and washed his hands before sitting down at table. First he took off his watch and rolled up his sleeves. One could see that only his youth prevented his forearms' being matted with hair. As it was, there was already a shadow creeping down as far as the knuckles of his hands. Above his eyes as they looked into the clouded shaving mirror, there were six or seven nascent wrinkles over which, unless he had just combed it, black curls fell spiraling on the warm skin. He might not have been good looking by some standards. It was the vital warmth of his appearance and the slightly worried earnestness which, alloyed with the native gaiety of his expression, gave him an air of candor, of goodness, through which the rascal showed as through a crystal.

"Giovanni, come and eat now." His mother spoke English to please him and he softened towards her. Nonetheless, he edged as far as possible from both his parents at table. His father's sour wine-breath made him angry and he could hardly take the garlic-laden food into his mouth. The thought that *she* might have smelt it as they passed each other that afternoon made him wince.

Of what had happened once he got upstairs to the room at the top of No. 7, Giovanni thought quite casually. Everyone knew about such people, and if that was what the old fool wanted and was willing to pay for, well that was all right, O.K. Strange to think, nonetheless, of how sick he'd felt afterwards. He'd gotten up in a hurry and slammed the bathroom door behind him. A thin, sweet water had come into his mouth and he had had to swallow many times. Then finally he'd felt better and come out to find the room empty and the watch lying on top of his jacket. On the way downstairs again he had had an adventure. A door which he had not noticed before stood open, and in it was the silhouette of a woman. The thing that struck him first was the whiteness of her skin—unnatural and inhuman. He had not seen her until they were right up close together and he had started.

"Jesus, you scared me!" he had exclaimed.

She had smiled, or made some kind of grimace, and put out her hand as if to detain him. He had the vague impression she wanted him to reassure her of her own existence, that she wanted to ask: "It *is* me, isn't it?" but she drew back her hand and he went on down, opened the door and breathed in the damp, cold city air. He could not have told her anyway. She did not look very real to him.

Mr. Puchini belched and loosened his belt. His mouth shone with oil beneath its mustache. Mrs. Puchini started clearing, moving her great bulk neatly around the table and sighing from overweight. She was still not thinking of everyday things, was still inside the tent, feeling over—self-conscious, ruffled and intrigued. The fortuneteller with his white hair and metal-flavored voice intrigued her and she regarded her kitchen with indifference. The cards certainly knew. They knew more about her than she did herself, or her husband, who had been with her for so many years. They told her things she felt but had never realized before.

Mr. Puchini put up his feet on the table and opened a movie magazine. He never went to the movies yet he loved to look at the photographs of the actresses. The long legs, in bathing suits or shorts, made his masculine ego rise. So much womanhood in America, so much perpetual girlhood, all put out for man, smiling at man, at Mr. Puchini representing man; sticking out hard, uplifted breasts, exposing the soft backs of thighs and looking over coy shoulders. Personally he preferred starlets to stars. He had an idea they would be sweeter, more submissive.

"Say, Giovanni, come here and look at this. Did you ever see such a shape like-a-this? What you think, is natural?"

Mrs. Puchini rattled the pots and pans in her kitchen, steam filled the flat, and Giovanni found himself suddenly perfectly contented.

"Sure, Pa," he said, coming over to look. "It's natural all right—natural rubber."

5

NOW THAT THE BACK of winter was broken there were a few marvelous days soft and clear as spring. One could smell the ozone in the air. Such a day had different effects on all the Tudelos household. It made Charles mean. It made Candy dreamy and Josie sentimental. It made the priest squeeze his hands together and it made Sheila weep. This last was only normal, since she wept every day.

Sheila, rising late in her untidy bedroom with its numerous cushions, hastily powdered her face, using a flattened puff. She had a mania about powder and could not stand to see her face without it. She went into her bathroom and ran the hot water until it came near to overflowing. She stepped into the tub with her narrow, white feet and a shudder contracted her skin into goose flesh. Then the whole surface of her body relaxed and softened. At such moments it felt precious, the white, heavy trunk, the slender legs, and it hurt her that such a treasure was discarded before it had ever really been used. Then, sitting in the water, she sobbed and the tears ran down the powder she had already put on her face.

Up to the base of her neck Sheila's coloring was delicate and pale as the inside of a shell. She was almost a redhead and had that quality of skin. There was no green or yellow in the undertones, and all the shadows—crook of arm or of knee, crevice of the body—were pink. The rusty brush of her pubic hairs stuck out between her legs, unkinked by the hot water.

Often when Sheila got out of the tub she felt too weak to dry herself and wandered around hardly knowing what she was doing. Sometimes a wave of blackness made her head spin, because the bath had been too hot and she had stayed too long in it. The imprints of her feet were all over the rug, dark wet patches, proof of the aimlessness of her mornings. Sheila hated this hour of the day—the time around eleven-thirty. Charles was still sound asleep. Her child was occupied and the hours stretched endlessly ahead. The ruling passion of her life was Charles, of course, so there was nothing to do until he woke up. Finally she would hear the scurryings, the ringings, the cracked oaths that signaled his awareness of a new day. Then Sheila's heart would start to beat and she would find her hands cold and her mouth dry.

'Do I really love him that much?' Sheila asked herself at times. She could never answer. She might not have heard the answer anyway; surely the beat of her heart ringing in her ears would have muffled the reply. He was a habit with her, a drug of longing and pity. This last word would have surprised her, yet it was true. One pitied him as one pities a cross unruly child who does not know what it wants and has worn itself out with its own ill-temper.

Sheila could recall happiness with her husband: those three days of it, and that sweet, unforgettable kiss on the mouth. Ah, to think of it now! Sometimes, sitting idly at her dresser or on her chaise longue, Sheila went over the time of their betrothal and early marriage. The lost hours were like ghosts that came to knock softly at her breast. And Sheila let them in. They were dead, but she could not reconcile herself to the living. Those few ghosts were all she could really bear now to welcome inside her heart, her poor, narrow, fretted heart.

Sixteen years ago Sheila and Charles had met in New York. She was a wealthy girl of twenty-seven and he a handsome young gigolo who appeared younger than he was and had been claiming twenty-five for quite a few seasons. Of course when he met Sheila he switched forward three years, out of gallantry. He was very gallant. She was taken with him at once and thought herself lucky to be seen with such a pair of pointed shoes and such suave dancing style. She, the bluestocking, the long of face, the near redhead. American men had, so far, let her politely alone, and although there were one or two pretendants, they were old or colorless. Not one—nobody she had ever seen, in fact—had so much vivacity and dash. How awkward she felt beside him! Even his waist was smaller than hers, yet he was so generous, so full of the most delicate attentions and compliments. They were engaged within a fortnight and the resulting storms and protests had gone over her head like wind.

Sheila's family, seeing they could not stop the marriage, had made the best of a bad bargain by holding fast to that part of her money that they had in trust. They were a family of big businessmen: jovial, loud, even honest, although judging from the fortune they had made, it was hard to believe. Sheila was a rarity among them, for their loins were almost incapable of producing girls, and for that reason she might have been spoiled and cherished. Her own awkward, shy nature got in the way of this, however, and besides, they liked flashy women. Had Sheila been one of those little girls who climb upon fathers' and uncles' knees with impudence and give them sideways looks, who insist on curlers at night, and wind their mothers' furs around their bodies—Ah then, what a success she would have been! No need to marry Charles then. Alas, she had been hopeless, and without even a business sense to attract their admiration. They just could not be bothered with her until her mesalliance had shocked them into temporary attention.

Now she hardly ever saw them at all, although formal letters came to the Duke when he had overstepped her income.

It was curious, and Sheila remembered it well, that a week before the wedding Charles himself had developed scruples. It was at a party given for the engaged couple by that woman Leonine. How cultured and fascinating Sheila had thought her in those days, her guests, too—handsome men looking like boys, and the women, many of them titled, with feline walks. She had never had such a good time. Then, all at once, Charles had pulled her out on the balcony and, looking at her with those sad, black eyes of his in which the lids already drooped, said:

"Sheila, I cannot let you go on. You do not know me—what I am."

His foreign accent broke the words so that they touched her keenly. She trembled with emotion. "My dear, I know you are you, that you are wonderful, that I love you."

"But I am a gigolo!" he cried. "Do you know what that means? I live off my wits, off women and off—" Here he stopped, struck by her face: the misty features of a woman in love, who does not listen, who shivers with love and innocence to the marrow of her bones. It was something he had never seen before and would probably never see again. Charles was repulsed. All his scruples left him. He leaned forward and kissed her mouth, opening his lips on hers and forcing his tongue between her teeth, and he felt the great spasm that shook her at his first caress. In all their married life, their child's birth, the secrets of their nuptials, he never kissed her on the mouth like that again.

The three happy days happened after the birth of Candy. Charles was delighted and sat at Sheila's bedside from morning to night, frequently taking her hand and squeezing it as he spoke of their future happiness with their beautiful child.

When the baby was brought in, he fairly danced with joy and insisted she nurse it at her breast while he was in the room. He would have liked all his friends to be present. One felt that it was a sorrow to him that his own nipples were useless. Candy, in those days, lived in dreams and looked at her parents without seeing them. Her blue eyes reflected backwards, to before her birth, perhaps to before her conception, and she gave secret smiles that drove her father wild. She had not been born with a caul, which was a pity, but her body was covered with black down like a little faun's.

Sheila was not maternal. All the emotion in her body was taken up already by her obsession for her husband, and it was just this which put a stop to the three happy days. In fact, she grew jealous of this baby. All at once, on the fourth morning, she woke up jealous, and when her husband came in, smiling and longing to see his child again, Sheila turned her face to the wall and said in her petulant, high-pitched voice:

"I understand it all now. You just want to see her! I might as well be a machine." And she added bitterly: "Now you've made her, you won't care anymore. I suppose you'll be wanting separate rooms."

Charles was staggered by his wife's insight and by her outspokenness, for it was rarely that she said a thing as it lay in her mind. In less than a year his own complexity had made her obtuse. He reacted by flushing crimson with rage and shouting:

"My God, you are complicated!"—which was exactly what she was not being. "Can't I have a simple pride in my first child without your making a Greek tragedy? My dear, you are very perverse!"

He had stamped around the room, going on and on in the same vein and she had listened with a mixture of triumph and pain, because the more he raged and waxed sarcastic, the more she knew she was right and knew further that she had hit upon a sore point. Or rather that she had anticipated what he had been thinking of since her pregnancy. More than this, he now hoped to lavish on his daughter openly a tenderness he would not give his wife—or was afraid to give her lest she demand more.

Sheila had let Charles rage and had spoken silently to herself: 'Yes, all the time he was in here billing and cooing, he was leading up to separate rooms.' He hoped her child would take up all her attention and leave him free of her, did he? Well, to revenge herself she resolved not to care about it at all and from that day refused to bother with the child further or even to nurse it.

After her burst of frankness to Charles and to her own self, Sheila had retired once more into her pointless scenes and evasions. Oh they had their separate rooms now! Indeed, Charles had a whole house where she might never enter. Sheila's mind shrank back at the thought of those unknown rooms, which she imagined to be dark and close. Although she often stood there at the threshold, the idea of going beyond the double door frightened her. Sometimes, though, she would say to the Duke:

"I think I'll go and take a look at the top floor of No. 7 today. I want another little chair in my room and perhaps I shall find it there."

Then her husband would raise his eyes with their drooping lids and look into her face for an instant before replying: "Do as you wish, *cherie.*" He knew as well as she did that it was idle talk.

She would continue, as before, to wait in her room between tears and repowdering, to leave on the floor those wet narrow idle traces, and to spend the forenoon listening for his voice. She heard it now. The door of the bedroom opened suddenly to admit Charles attired in a grey suit and an oversized bow tie.

"Not dressed!" he cried. "But, *cherie,* I asked Dee-dee and Nano for lunch. You knew I had my reasons."

"I don't feel very well today." Sheila did not even look at her husband now that he had come, although she had been waiting for him and listening for his voice all morning.

It was always the same between this husband and wife; they paid and repaid each other in equal coinage." First it was he who would not act the host, and then she. It infuriated Charles the more because it was not natural in Sheila, but a trick she had copied from him. Go without guests in his house, he could and would not; and he wanted Sheila to be its continual lady in order that he might come and go as he wished. He was far too unstrung to stay in one room with one set of people. He must do a thousand other things: telephone, listen to new records, swallow benzedrine, even go out to a night club with some of his guests. But he wanted a crowd to be there all evening in his long narrow salon, to owe the evening to him and to take up the time of his house. His wife's attitude drove him to despair.

"For years I have slaved to make ours the greatest salon in New York. When we married you did not know how to greet people or what to say to men and women of culture. *I* have made you and this is how you reward me!"

"But I never said I wanted a salon." The little bird flew feebly up and away from Sheila's throat.

Charles was brought to a standstill. Of course, it was true, Sheila had never wanted a salon. She had never wanted anything he had given her, or rather transformed for her, out of her proper wealth. She did not care for clothes, or jewels, or witty society. She wanted him. It was not fair, thought Charles. He had paid dearly enough for the pleasure of being rich without this constant, sick, thwarted longing. When would it end? When would this large, soft femaleness dry up and turn away from him and let him alone to torture his own heart in peace? He lost his temper.

The vein in his neck filled and pressed against his collar. Sheila observed the sign and repressed a little smile. Then, all at once, as if recalling something, Charles breathed out quietly. His eyes, half hooded, grew remote, almost gentle.

"Comme tu veux, cherie. Perhaps if you stayed in bed a little while—" His hand was on the knob and before she could acquiesce he was gone once more.

Her husband's collapse was the worst revenge he could have taken, and in five minutes after he left the room Sheila was consumed by the frustration that could have been eased by his anger. She could not sit still and thought of a hundred petty quarrels she had had with Charles, of a hundred replies she might have made. Then, too, behind each scene of theirs, there was the superficial reason and the real, deep reason. What, for instance, was the real reason why he had given in just now? Sheila's teeth were on edge; she could have broken the enamel off the ends of them. Her handkerchief was a ball in her hands.

'I just can't stand it any longer,' she thought. 'I shall leave the house and not come back until midnight. How furious and frightened he will be!'—And so Charles would have been, had Sheila ever carried out this simple threat.

She got dressed, threw on her dowdy-looking clothes, dusted over already by the white powder with which she was continually powdering her face. Someone knocked and then Candy entered. She was fresh and pale, with her hair pulled back and rather a pinched look. She had just finished lunch in her room.

"Good morning, Mama. How do you feel this morning? Papa said you were not well."

"Oh, so you saw your father?"

"Just for a moment." Candy realized that she was in the intolerable position of having her mother jealous of her relations with her father. She knew, too, that although there could have been companionship between Charles and herself, it had been ruthlessly sacrificed by her father so that his more important affections could be satisfied. There had to be an offering, an obvious one, a calf led to the altar with much ceremony. Candy the immaculate, the beautiful, Candy of the long eyes that never wept. Sheila looked at the sacrifice without pity from under her moist, red lids.

"Mama," said Candy, "may I not have my music lessons back?"

"Well," answered Sheila uncertainly, "I don't know. Your father said Lee was really a very dishonest person and that he had found out things about him that made it impossible. So I don't see—" Under Candy's calm gaze she became confused. They both knew that Lee Kahn's offense was different from these hints. In No. 7, among those dark passageways, those close rooms, some drama had been played.

"It's all right, Mama," said Candy.

Sheila was putting on her hat. Candy came over and deftly adjusted its short veil.

6

* *Candy's diary:*

...... My little diary, how oppressed I feel today. The weather is dull and I meander around my room when I should be doing my lessons. The smell of open sewers seems to come in at the sash of my window. How slow the workmen are! One holds a wedge and another drives it in. The tar surface of the road cracks.

He is no longer among them. Do they know why? Do I?

These days I hardly ever come to meals. Josie brings them to me here in my room. Mama does not want me at meals. I am too big and I take up too much of the guests' attention, or rather of Papa's. Papa would like to have me but there are other things he wants more. So now, you see, he can hold me up as an example of Mama getting her way. My music teacher is gone. He was silly and shy but better than nothing. I have no amusements now other than my dreams. Last night I dreamt I was in a garden in a foreign city. Rome? Who knows. I was tired and it was a boiling summer day. I was wearing a thin dress that stuck to my legs as I walked all alone down an alley, through a high, rusty gate into the garden. The gate squeaked frightfully. Why could I hear it so plainly if it was only a dream? Inside everything was drooping in the afternoon heat. The big trees trailed their branches down on the lawn which was untended and full of weeds. There was a fountain in the center, not spouting, but pouring out through the mouth of a mask. Pouring down fitfully into a stone basin. Beside the garden was a house.......

* * *

Candy paused in her writing and leaned back. Her dream became real to her in the writing of it. She walked again in the garden between its high walls. With its uncut grass, its vine-choked flowers, it spoke of nostalgia and desertion. Only the birds and the insects flew about, and several trees cast their shadows like gifts onto the ground. Through the mouth of the mask the water ran in a flat stream—a foreign tongue murmuring among strangers. She was diverted by the beauty of that stone face and went nearer to examine it. It was that of a cyclops whose lips, opened and drawn down to let the fountain through, seemed to express a continual scorn and pain. In the middle of the broad, troubled forehead, above the nose with its sensual nostrils, its tormented root, the single eye of the cyclops glared out unblinking at the wilderness. The eyeball was red with a black circle in the center, the only color in the whole face. Candy leaned curiously across the basin and touched the eye with her finger. It was warm from the afternoon sun.

She sat on the edge of the basin and looked up at the house. The sun moved behind it, leaving it grey and sinister. She noticed on the second floor that one of the windows was broken. There was a black hole, a wound, in the somber stone.

All at once Candy started to her feet. She thought she had seen a face staring down.

That was as far as the dream had taken her. One always woke up in places like that. Candy sat forward and continued writing:

* * *

I think I have been in that garden when I was very young, or perhaps it is still in the future. Somehow I feel I know the person in the window. And the mask is trying to speak, perhaps give me the most urgent message. I don't understand what it wants to say. Will I ever understand? Am I being stupid? Do I live too much alone? Well, I shan't always. Someday I shall be rich and free, as well they know. What a lot of things people know in this house of which they never speak. For instance, *I* know what happens in No. 7!

* * *

At this point Candy snapped the book shut and locked it with its gold key.

"Josie!" she called, "Josie!" But the maid was elsewhere and no one answered. She opened the door of her room and listened to the buzzing noise made by her father's guests two floors below. Their voices were sifted and changed by polished stairways, by carpets and by thick, caking lipstick. They floated up and filled her silent virgin's room. By putting her hand to her cheek, she could feel the coldness of her fingers which seemed slowly to freeze the blood throughout her body. She stepped outside into the hall and then looked back.

'Of course it doesn't mean anything. I've often gone there before,' she thought, forming the last phrase aloud. But as if to belie these words, the light from her bedroom windows struck from her eyes a hard, glittering spark. She faced forward once again and walked to the stairhead. Putting her hand on the rail, she skimmed down like a maimed bird, one of those solitary sea birds who break their wings occasionally on the violent current of the storm. She ran through her father's office, through the deserted bedroom, and through the double door.

There the other house waited for her and was dark. Not a sound came to her ears, yet she got the impression that someone had passed by very recently. Old houses retain such footsteps on their floors. Old houses grow tense with waiting and are impregnated by the tempers of their guests. Anger throws a red light in their corners. Tears seep into their woodwork and corrode the stranger's hand.

Candy drank in the breath of this passing and gazed thoughtfully about. Had there ever been a time when she had not foreseen today? Now that she was actually in No. 7, there was no need to hurry. She felt dragged down by the weight of her intentions. Candy was afraid, a cold, physical fear that made her steps falter.

Giovanni was sitting idly on the bed in the front, topfloor bedroom and he responded to the light tapping on his door with a sulky invitation:

"Come in." When he saw who it was, he started and leapt to his feet. "Why Miss Candy!"

"How do you know my name?"

"I—I just heard."

Candy walked up to him and put her hand lightly on his breast. A blush swelled Giovanni's veins until his head itself seemed to grow bigger. All his features became blurred. Blue lines filled the hollows of his temples. His mouth looked stung as by a venomous insect. Even the eyes, beneath his fine silky lashes, were shot with blood.

"Giovanni," said Candy, and as though it had been a command, he fell to his knees. The thud of his bones against the floor made him bite his tongue so hard that tears came to his eyes and he lowered his head an instant.

"Giovanni," she said again, and then: "Get up, Giovanni. We don't have much time."

He raised his face at that and the tears had fallen on his cheeks. He put his square, dark hands with their broken nails over the mounds of her knees.

"Should I take off my clothes?" asked Candy.

"Miss Candy, I don't—we can't—" And he cried despairingly. "What would your father say?"

The girl, who had at first been softened by his tears and by the tenderness of his position, now turned away her face at his words. The too small ears, the flat twist of her head, had for an instant a snakelike look. "It's up to you," she said. "How should *I* know what to do?"

A hint of mockery or contempt in her voice brought the boy out of his indecision in an instant. He felt nothing but anger, a flaming anger that was almost hatred. On his knees, with tears running down his face! How ridiculous he must appear! Ah, he would show her it was no joke to be alone with him, Giovanni, and the door shut. His expression became ugly and he rose to his feet in a supple movement. Candy remained quietly in front of him, but as he started to unbutton her schoolgirl's blouse, she once again put her hand lightly against his breast. The quiet, light touch ate into his skin like hot sealing wax; a seal stamped into his heart, burnt into it. By the time she was in her slip he could stand it no longer, but taking hold of the white cotton stuff, tore it from end to end, snatching with it the rest of her clothing so that she was left naked all at once. Then Giovanni gave a great, gasping cry. He really thought he was stifling and, as if to ease his congestion, threw himself upon her so that she fell beneath him to the floor.

Giovanni was never, even at best, a good lover. He was healthy, lighthearted and selfish. That was all. What a woman felt, or experienced, meant nothing to him. With a sure egoism he imagined she could only be grateful. Whether Candy was grateful or not, he never knew. After it was over she got up and, with her odd mixture of the arrogant and the awkward, put on her clothes. Crouching on his thick, flexible thighs, Giovanni could not look at her and stared instead at the carpet where she had lain. He himself was fully dressed. He saw her hand as it reached down to pick up her torn underclothes and he saw her two long, slender feet in their brown oxfords slightly toeing in.

"Goodbye, Giovanni," she said, ready to go. And as he lifted his head, she gave him her marvelous glance unravished. Outside, Candy walked as fast as possible while pressing the torn underclothes between her legs. She started reviewing the secret places in her room because she would have things to hide in future. The little gold key, for instance, must be hidden now for fair!

Giovanni meanwhile got up and paced about, smoking a cigarette. His mind was also occupied with hiding. His stocky form, in shirt and trousers, looked suddenly cowardly and furtive. Whenever he came to the window, he looked down on the heads of his former companions working in the construction. It seemed to him they did not work very hard. He saw them joking and laughing, leaning often on their tools. He would have liked to go down there and force them to cut out their nonsense. Regan was too lax. Now if he were in Regan's position—He frowned and stamped back to the place in the carpet where he had lain with Candy. It was near the bed, in plain view of the doorway. He stooped, touched it with his hand and put his forefinger to his mouth. The bitter, salty taste was mixed with dust. He tried to picture Candy as she must have appeared, standing naked in front of him. Since she was very young her body was surely hardly developed, yet he could form no image in his brain. He recalled only that her thighs did not meet at top but left a space, giving her the touching, ugly look that belongs to those one loves dearly.

A noise from the floors below made Giovanni start. Was it the Duke? It was time to act, in any case. He ran to the adjoining bathroom and took the thin drinking glass above the wash basin. Coming back to the spot between bed and door, he debated a moment, shifting the glass from hand to hand, trying to recall something. Then his face cleared and, contracting his hand, he broke the glass to pieces in his palm. The jagged edges pierced and stayed in his flesh.

Giovanni stood there, listening to the sound of steps on the stair and holding his lacerated hand above the carpet. Years ago, as a boy, he had cut his wrist for an initiation and in a strange way he felt that rite completed now. Two events in his life bound together by blood. He saw in his mind's eye the dirty little boy by the river, cutting his wrist boldly so that others would not think him afraid.

With Giovanni's blood went all his anger, his lust and his pain, purged from him more surely than by his seed.

Charles came in and saw the boy standing still, holding the wrist of his left hand with his right so that thick, red drops oozed onto the carpet.

"I broke a glass," said Giovanni, "and I'm bleeding."

Charles looked at him from his heavy eyes and said wearily, but with irritation: "Poor baby!" He was irritated at the thought that his pleasures might be disturbed and something in the atmosphere of the room filled him with a sort of sad fretfulness.

"You must wash it at once, idiot!" he cried, reassembling his energies. *"Regarde le done!* Standing like an ox with the pieces of glass still in his skin! I let you stay up here alone five minutes and you play the fool!—*Mais ne reste pas comme ca!* Move, can't you?" Charles was now in a tantrum. The constant drip, drip of blood on the floor obscurely terrified him and got on his nerves. There was something in the boy's expression too, stupid and sly. "Go and wash!" he screamed and then, without waiting to be obeyed, he strode forward and, seizing the wounded hand, squeezed with all his might.

Their two pairs of eyes were close together now. Giovanni's were closed in anguish. The Duke's were half open. Beneath the impaired and twitching muscles of the lids they had not lost their brooding expression.

7

MRS. PUCHINI WOKE with a start to find the darkness pressing in around her. She woke in fear, the terror that can grip a human soul at night.

Mr. Puchini snored lightly beside his wife and she raised herself up a bit on the pillows. A stab, as of a sharp instrument, sent a pang through the upper part of her left arm and at once she felt it again: fear! With her hand she explored the place where it hurt. Of course there was nothing there. From the harsh, black pit beneath her arm to the horny elbow bump, the skin was unmarred, a solid skein of fat and muscle. Why then this sensation, this lonely pain while everyone else slept? Ah, but she knew the source. To rehearse it brought her to a kind of abject and primitive cringing, almost to pleasure.

Because her adventure had not ended in the tent on the little cross-street. Since then the fair had closed. The carrousel had gone to the country, the Punch and Judy show back to Greenwich village, and the fortuneteller to his room on West Seventy-sixth Street. But before leaving, he had given her his card with the name *Neju* written in red and the words *Palmist and Seer* underneath in black.

"Come soon," he had said, adding: "While there is still time."

Needless to say, Mrs. Puchini had gone. The house where Neju lived was set narrowly between garages and stables, a dingy brownstone. The landlady had looked the Italian woman over shrewdly when she had said at the door:

"Mr. Neju, please, is appointment."

"Oh, don't worry about that. He's got time, and he's not *Mr.* Neju, just Neju. Right up to the top and to your left."

Neju's room had been different from what she expected, very neat, almost fussy, as though he had been one of those threadbare old maids fallen on hard times. The curtains had been drawn against the afternoon sun and there was a constant knocking and hissing from the radiator in the corner. It was too warm up there and she was forced either to keep on her coat and perspire or take it off and show the straining cloth at bosom and thigh. Nonetheless, she visited him again and paid him, too, and grew more and more dependent on his counsel. It was strange that after one of these visits to Neju, Mrs. Puchini could never quite recall what he had told her to do about the dangers which menaced her. She only knew that the dangers existed and were, he assured her, far worse than anything she had feared.

At about her fourth visit Neju looked up from the cards and said: "You are wasting my time," and as she started to reply, he cut her off coldly: "You are not co-operating. If you wish the Supreme Power, through me, to help you, you must become receptive. You must put aside your will and let the Master Spirit enter into you."

The poor woman felt she was doing wrong. "I pray to God each night," she said. "Every night before I sleep I pray to Him. I *am* what you call—receptive—to Him."

"I am not talking about God," the man answered, and his voice with its metallic ring sent a shiver into her flesh.

Mrs. Puchini hung her head and, as she felt his eyes on her gross misshapen limbs, turned scarlet and began to itch. Even in his room he made her sit on the little round stool that caused her to be ridiculous. Yet he never said a word to which she could object, and even if he had, she must by now have taken it in silence. Besides, she knew that he did not desire her in the least, and was all the more uneasy. She came to understand as well, although he did not say so in words, that his Supreme Power was the devil, the Prince of Darkness. But so long as he called no spirit by name, she soothed herself into acquiescence.

Nonetheless, Neju felt her will standing feebly up against his own and set out to crush it.

"There is a pain inside you like a spider," he said, "and no doctor can cure it. Its name alone means incurable, rotting, putrescence, death! Like a spider it will stretch its legs and spray poison from its entrails into yours."

Mrs. Puchini trembled with fear, as much from his choice of phrases as from their import. She begged him to advise her, to help her, as she was convinced he could do, and he shuffled the cards and started laying them out anew.

All at once he stopped and cried harshly: "You see! You are resisting me. You had better go away and return no more."

The woman burst into tears of nervousness and fear. "I do everything you tell me. I no understand!"

He appeared to relent slightly. "Well, well, I will think of a way. Dry your tears and come back in two days. It will be all right. Just do as I say," and he added in a different tone: "A big woman like you—crying!"

The next time she came he greeted her with a smile. "I am working a way out of our difficulties," he told her.

Then, taking both her hands, he looked at the palms in silence for a few minutes. "You see," he said, "your left palm is clear and simple, easy to read, but your right is full of petty worries, hesitancies and stubbornness. The left is the character and fate to which you were born. The right is how you have willfully molded your life. In it are children, husband, marketing, migration, priests—a hundred things to trouble you, to stop the Supreme Power, the spirit, from passing into you. You have made yourself into a muddy, thick clay, whereas you must become fluid and transparent as water."

As Neju spoke, he looked her up and down almost tenderly so that she could feel her thick body stopping him and wished with all her heart she could please him better. "I want you to be simple and clear," he continued. "You must put yourself entirely in my hands. Under my control and, through me, under *his* control."

Neju's tones had grown increasingly severe as he scanned her right hand, the palm of which was puffy and overpink. Mrs. Puchini understood very little of these phrases. She tried desperately to know what he wanted of her and her face puckered with anxiety.

Suddenly he cried: "Yes, yes, there it is again, danger! All your resistance cannot stop me from seeing that."

"But what can I do? Ah, Maria, you no tell! I not know!"

Her distress must have touched him for he said: "Now, now, it is grave, but there *is* a way. I have made a little figure, your likeness, in wax. This will help us work together. It will help my will to get in touch with, to master, yours."

As he pronounced the words 'to master,' Mrs. Puchini felt chilled. She was born in an old country and knew of such practices although they went against her religion. How had she put herself in this position? God was known to disapprove and to chastise. As though he read her thoughts of revolt, Neju looked at her sharply and she took his whole aspect in recoil. The old-young face beneath white hair, the faint, pinched lines around the mouth, the metallic voice, all disgusted her. Yet she was strangely medieval. Her childhood in an ancient city, her church, the pattern of her married life, had combined to give her—or perhaps to make her aware of—a living soul. Terrible and terrifying thing, to have a soul, to have it in the hands of Neju!

Several days later, in the nighttime, Mrs. Puchini felt the first sharp prick.

"That's good!" cried Neju when he questioned her. "That shows you are getting more submissive. You must become like the wax of your image," and he showed her a squat little doll in a black dress through which a pin was thrust. The doll had real hair on its head, a few straight, black strands. Mrs. Puchini's one remaining pride was her jet hair unmixed with white.

Now the woman dared no longer show resentment or recoil. She smiled at the charlatan humbly with trembling lips, sitting awkwardly on the stool that was so small, that cut a scarlet circle in her flesh. Yet, with all her horror, there was mingled the pleasure of surrender, that sweet pleasure that so few women can resist. She who had never done anything before that she had not told to a priest now no longer went to confess. Her few, oft-repeated prayers became sacrilege on her lips. She fancied that although she formed the words correctly they changed the minute they were in the air. Surely they became the abracadabra of sorcery! Then she would start from her knees and pray no more.

The bittersweet terror fretted Mrs. Puchini day and night. She would lie awake and know Neju was awake too, pricking with a pin the soft, frail wax. He was like a drug to her now, and the days she did not see him were full of anxiety. Yet he was not always free and he became increasingly harsh.

So on this night, before dawn, the obsessed woman woke and, feeling the sharp twinge in her left arm, decided she must go tomorrow at all costs, though it was not yet the date set for her next visit.

It was past two in the afternoon before she set out. Her husband had returned home for lunch and she could hardly conceal the restlessness that so ill became her two hundred-odd pounds. Even Mr. Puchini gave her a surprised look or two as he ate. Afterwards she caught the bus across town, sitting in the rear and watching the streets lurch by. Central Park was hidden by walls, but she could smell the damp, melting snow, the dirty, stagnant water from its ponds. At the Columbus Avenue bus stop she got out and walked, setting her feet down heavily in the slush. The day before there had been a temporary thaw, and now the gutters were trickling while the streets and sidewalks were coated with a thin, brown slime. Here and there a pile of snow remained black and porous to infect the air. The dampness penetrated clothing and caused the ears to open and close painfully. From one instant to the next Mrs. Puchini heard the traffic grow unbearably sharp or else as dim as a dream.

When she reached her goal, she was chilled through and the landlady's face twisted with spite at her bulbous red nose and cracked lips.

"Neju ain't in." She closed the door to a mere crack and through this Mrs. Puchini could see an eye, half curious and half suspicious. The landlady hoped for a question, a plea of some sort, but life and the bearing of children had given the Italian woman a patience which was stronger than nerves. She said nothing and turned away, down the brownstone steps, and the landlady had either to close the door or get a chill.

Mrs. Puchini waited on the sidewalk for hours. Occasionally she walked up and down, when her anguish made her incapable of standing still. For she was in anguish. That he was out, sent her into a panic. Out! While she—the living soul of her, the ghost flesh of her—was trapped in his room I Where had he gone, and suppose something happened to him? The cold, raw afternoon darkened and a gloomy dusk crept across the park like an animal. Working girls and men passed by; horses from the nearby stables, and the dirty, west-side children with their hoarse voices. All seemed to her to be blissfully going home to light and warmth. Only she, by some cruel destiny, must stand and wait. Her heart the while, like one of her own dishcloths, was wrung and unwrung inside her breast.

Finally, after the streets were already lit, she saw him coming, his head up and muttering excitedly to himself. He would have gone on up the steps without even noticing her, so she touched his arm timidly.

"Mr. Neju!"—she had never got over calling him Mister—"Please, I want-a-to ask-a-you—I mean I want—" What *did* she want? Now that he was here she felt ashamed of her panic, absurdly relieved by the very sight of him.

Neju had jumped at her touch and now cut in with: "I'm busy. You had no appointment today." He had been thinking of his own problems and was angry at being seen first. Then, as she was about to turn humbly away, he delayed her: "Wait!"

The woman faced him again and he could just make out the round moons of her cheeks in the semidarkness. He sucked his lip, still undecided, and then: "Yes, wait. I have something I wish to tell you. Come in. We cannot discuss it here."

On the way upstairs they were both silent except for her breathing and the creak of her readymade corsets. She was acutely aware of him behind her, viewing her monstrous shapes made even more ridiculous by foreshortening. At each step she felt the displacement of her flesh and the bulge of her thigh that quivered as the corset cut in above it. She would have liked to beg him to pass her and go on ahead and was faint with shame. When at last they reached his room, she could not force herself to stop panting, yet even so she sensed a difference in the man, an excitement. His voice, however, when he spoke, was controlled:

"Mrs. Puchini, you know by now that—" Then he stopped and made a violent gesture. What was the use of suave words and explanations. She was in his power and must do as he asked. He flicked his tongue over the edge of his lips and gathered himself together like a cat about to pounce. Rising to his feet, he fixed her with that Nordic stare which, since Viking days, has been able to subdue Latin women. "Mrs. Puchini," he said, "next time you come, tomorrow to be precise, you will bring with you five hundred dollars—in cash."

This was so little what she had expected to hear that the woman sat there completely dumb. Neju must have fancied she protested, because he raised his voice as though he were cutting in on her words: "Yes, you will bring it, Mrs. Puchini. Because tonight I shall take the little image I have made, *your* image, with your hair on its head and your aches in its bones. I shall put it right there, on top of the radiator. Look!" He sprang across the room, seized the wax doll from its hiding place and thrust it face down on the top of his radiator.

Mrs. Puchini gave a cry of horror, clasping her hands. The whole front of her face and body was shocked and bruised as though she herself had been flung down thus.

"Oh, don't be afraid." Neju smiled. "The heat is turned off and I won't turn it on until tomorrow." Then it struck him that this big, stupid woman might not have understood. "Don't you see?" he cried, "You'll melt, *melt!*"

She opened her mouth as if to reply but no words came. He could see her tongue working awkwardly between her decaying teeth. Now Neju could no longer bear the sight of her. "Go, go. And remember I shall turn on the heat at nine a.m. tomorrow, so the sooner you arrive—with the five hundred dollars, of course—the better for you." He came up close to her and said forcefully and slowly: "After that you can have your precious doll. I'll give it to you. Yes, all you have to do is pay. I certainly shan't want it after that, nor it, nor you ever, ever again." He raked back his white hair and looked deridingly into her eyes. "Not a pleasant way to die, a big woman like you!"

The creature, for by now she was hardly anything else, got up and he guided her out the door. Solicitously he turned on the light at the top of the stair and then watched her heavy shadow flung against wall and landing as she descended.

8

WHEN HE HEARD the front door slam, away down at the bottom of the house, Neju gave a sigh. The quality of old-youngness in his face stood out. The dirty light of the boardinghouse hall gleaming on his head, or perhaps simply his inner state, caused one feature to war with another. It was as if youth and age had lived in him perfectly well until now and at this exact moment had seen that they were enemies after all.

Neju was one of those men to whom nature had given every trait belonging to good looks and had stopped there. The sacred breath had been withheld. Without it the features were cold, unpleasant, unable to find life. His hair had turned white before he was twenty, and he could recall finding a white hair at thirteen. In the beginning this had made for a certain amount of success; his beard did not come until late, and his voice—well, that metallic timbre might be taken for adolescence, together with a smooth skin.

He often wondered at what point in his career luck had started to desert him. Was it at twenty-eight, when Leonard dropped out of his life? Neju had been haughty then; plenty of other friends were only waiting for a chance at intimacy. Yet, when one came to it, none of them had been up to Leonard's mark. No, that was not quite correct. None of them had been up to the mark as far as he, Neju, was concerned, but some of them had risen since. There was, for instance, young Tudelos. No *de* then. Carlos Tudelos had placed himself permanently in safety by a rich marriage. Neju wondered if he could have done the same. Women, however, were dangerous, and rich ones, usually, more so than any. How Carlos had managed all these years one could not imagine. He had, though, and a recent experience of Neju's proved it.

The charlatan went into his room and closed the door wearily. Then he took the little waxen image from the top of the radiator because the heat was not really off and it had begun to melt. He looked at it for a few minutes, turning it in his pale hands, those hands to which the protruding veins never seemed to bring the real blood-warmth. The image *was* rather a good likeness. He had taken trouble with it and even a certain pleasure as he modeled the form of Mrs. Puchini and sewed the dress of cheap black stuff. The coarse contours of neck, nose, cheek and chin were also duplicated, small though the statue was. What with the heat from the radiator putting a gloss over all the visible wax and making the rest cleave to the material, it became almost unpleasantly good. As he had just seen her, for instance, sweating, ashamed and terrified.

Neju gave another sigh and threw his creation carelessly on the chair. A good likeness. There had been a time when that slight gift of his had seemed weapon enough to conquer the world. "And what do *you* do, Nigel? I *can* call you Nigel, can't I?"—"Oh, I'm a sculptor" (said with just the right shade of youthful deference)—"But how thrilling! *May* I see one day? You know if your work is anywhere as extraordinary as you are—" Well, he was no longer Nigel, he was Neju. Neju the palmist, the magician, the charlatan. The road down had been as slow and painful as some people's road up. A beardless cheek grows dry the sooner. A breaking voice sounds metal-thin before thirty. Where were all those friends, those lovers of pure art, of the Greek way? 'But I know where one of them is,' he thought. Tudelos was on top, and perhaps he, not Neju but Nigel once again, could take advantage of an old friendship.

Last Wednesday, that deceptively warm day which had caused the present slush, Neju had gone out to Broadway. It was a fact that he frequently picked up clients in the movies. Women went alone in the afternoon, bored women, ready to believe anything. It was quite easy. In the throng, for example, one was pushed roughly up against one of them. One apologized with a slight English accent, bound to make the victim look around favorably. An accent meant glamour and mystery, an English accent meant gentleman as well. Once eye to eye, one gave a start one quickly repressed. "Pardon me, Madame,"—said the European way—""I didn't mean to stare. It's abominably rude of me. I just suddenly saw you were going to have a tremendous stroke of luck. I'm always right, you know." The woman probably responded, and the rest followed routine. An appointment would be made and he would have another fish hooked. Yet women disgusted him, and he could not or would not keep a client long. And most men, if they went in for having their fortunes told, preferred gypsies, even if they were Neju's kind of men.

Last Wednesday Neju had felt especially discouraged. Since the fair had closed he could not seem to get back in the old groove. He simply did not feel up to approaching anyone. Finally it was he, himself, who got approached. A little birdlike voice in his ear twittered:

"Excuse me, could you tell me how to get to the Roxy? I thought it was around here somewhere. It did used to be. Perhaps it's changed."

Something in the voice turned Neju into Nigel at once. He left off all but a trace of his English accent and started giving directions. Then he made a desperate move. "I believe we've met before, haven't we?" Ah, it wasn't enough. He was aware of her shrinking. He cast about wildly in his mind for a name. "Could it have been at Carlos'—" No, they called him Charles now. "—Charles de Tudelos?"

The shrinking relaxed and she said: "Well, it might have been. We have so many people to our house that it's hard to keep track."

"What luck!" he cried immediately. "I *thought* I recognized you. I didn't quite dare say. It *is* so embarrassing to be wrong."

"Oh, I'm often wrong," she said, at the same time turning aside in the offhand manner which many frustrated people have and which is sometimes misinterpreted as rude or shy. She continued: "Well, thank you for directing me."

"But I can't let you go like this. Allow me at least to come with you as far as the Roxy and to see you safely inside."

Sheila, however, found the thought of walking beside him unpleasant. She hated to see people on the street and talk to them in plain daylight. She was instinctively afraid of what people might read in her countenance. Neju, who had had experience in such reading, had already taken in several details: the small dim eyes, the shrunken, untidy edge of veil across her nose, and the redhead's fleshy chin. This last especially showed up the marks of life upon this creature. A sign of original fervor, it was now much too white, with a dead heaviness of design. Yet there was about her the unmistakable stamp of wealth, the smell of idleness and ease, which he breathed with pleasure.

To get rid of him, she said: "No, no, don't bother to come with me. Another time—come to the house one day again."

He took his cue. "If you really don't wish it. I *did* have an appointment. But I'll take you up on that invitation one of these days."

"Yes do, do. Come some evening." Was she ever going to rid herself of this man whom she recognized as a leech and a climber? Sheila felt another instant would be too much. Like many women in her position, the man who had withheld himself had become her fetish and she could not bear to touch another. The thought of taking this stranger's hand and saying goodbye was rapidly growing impossible, yet she did not know how else they could part. In desperation she cried: "Why not come next Thursday evening," and with an ugly movement Sheila heaved her whole body around and fairly ran off.

Neju followed her with his eyes as far as he could in the crowd. Shrill voices filled the air. The horde of humanity around him was excited by the false caress of spring. Right in front of him a strolling couple began to kiss. Neju saw their parted mouths meet while their noses, chafed and raw from winter colds, dug into each other's cheeks. The woman's rigidly molded bosom pointed at the man like a weapon, although her hips were still turned forward. His arm around her waist half lifted her from the ground, and they walked so that her shoes slithered along the pavement, running over at the heel. A secret progression of the kiss made the woman giggle.

"Don't, Jack, not on the street!" They both looked automatically behind them at Neju. "You see," she said, "there's a guy right there, seeing it all!"

"Oh he don't mind. He must have done it plenty himself. I bet you he wishes he was me, though."

They had neither of them really noticed Neju and spoke as if he could only be pleased to look on at such a spectacle. The man was good looking, young, with a quantity of hair parted on the side—but the girl! What was there in that species with its softness, its strange proportions and, worst of all, its terrible air of *fitting?* Neju hated to be asking himself these questions. It made him angry in a painful, sick way. He turned hurriedly around and started to walk uptown. No, there was no use in questions: men answered only in banalities, and God never bothered to answer at all. Yet why, he thought to himself, why?

Whenever he was especially tired or upset in some way, Neju would find himself thinking of an incident of his very early youth which had never retired to the black, dim depths of that second, that other, brain whose movements and thought travail ceaselessly behind the first. He did not like to think of it; for some reason it seemed to be at the root of all his troubles. In any case, he thought of it only in troubled times.

It happened when he was between three and four—he could remember himself on and off since two—at a time when his family had been living on a farm in Massachusetts. His father, a silent, Nordic man, had nevertheless been extremely prolific and Neju was followed by a sister before the year was out. He must have been one of those creatures—easily recognized in cats especially—who have been weaned too soon. The craving to suckle had been among the earliest desires that he could recall. How he envied the little sister or brother who lay currently upon his mother's breast! Even the foals, the calves, and the lambs seemed to his baby mind to enjoy a bliss from which he was cut off. From his minute height the farm world had appeared to be filled with sweet, eager, uplifted mouths into which paradise was flowing. The sound of their sucking lips had resounded in his ears and he had grown thin and fretful in front of porridge.

One day while playing in the barn he had found Lotta, the big, whitish mongrel bitch, feeding her litter on the straw. He got down on his hands and knees and came up close to watch. Lotta had lain there smiling a little, with her tongue out, while the puppies tumbled and struggled at her tits. She looked at the child with a benevolent eye and let him crawl very close. Suddenly he could stand it no longer. Why should they, shapeless and ugly, have all the nectar of life while he thirsted? He buried his face convulsively in the shifting mass and found what he sought. His lips closed on it and he drew in Lotta's milk with all his might. He must have bitten her, or else the suction was too strong, for she gave a yelp and started up. The child, too, leapt to his feet and was overwhelmed by what he had done. The taste of the milk nauseated and terrified him. The bitch became a monster crawling with thick, white slugs. He started to scream and ran out of the barn, piercing the air with his cries until his mother came running out of the house to snatch him up in her arms. Pressed against the full mounds of her bosom, he screamed the louder, hitting out with his little fists, and she held him all the closer until he grew first silent and then deathly sick. The white froth had stained her throat and blouse.

Walking uptown, Neju relived all the nausea of those moments. He wished his inner brain would devour them and swallow them up so that they would be known to him no more. He sometimes scoffed at psychiatrists who forced the past memories out of their patients' minds into the open. Ah, if that memory of his were only lost, he would not have it found for a fortune! But had the harm really been done then, in that crude farm story, or had, before birth, some trick of feeding or of seed set his glands awry?

By this time Neju had arrived at Columbus Circle, a sordid corner bordering the park. Here could be seen any day of the week a kind of entertainment. Neju watched a bearded man walk past, his hair tied school-girl fashion at the nape of his neck. On reaching an accustomed spot, this false Christ drew off the string and let his hair fall down on his shoulders. He was going to preach. Nearby, in the center of a crowd, a crazy woman in sackcloth sang hymns. A rabble rouser spat saliva from his soapbox platform. These people and others filled the air with venom. Neju felt as one of them despite himself, felt tied to them all by the twist in his system and by the cruel baseness of his trade. And these people who shouted and raved, where did they stem from? What did they do when they left the Circle? What memories haunted them in weariness or despair? Perhaps, contrary to opinion, it was the very quality of repression that was needed for normality.—With a shrug of revolt Neju turned into Central Park where women and children were enjoying the late clear sunshine of the day..

'I must get out of it! I will,' he muttered half aloud and he resolved to go to the Duke's house. 'Money attracts money,' he thought, 'and who knows what may not come to me once I am among people of means.' Yet something in this thought disturbed him and he sat down on a bench to reflect. Yes, money attracted money, but was he fit to go as he was? He was badly dressed. He smelt, surely, of boardinghouse stairs and cheap soap and, what was worse, he had an impossible address. How fully he realized now the depths to which he had sunk! A wave of rage and anguish contorted his features. He cast his mind with hatred over his few miserable clients. Vulgar, stupid women whom he tried his best to render hysterical. Shoddy and poor as well. They merited any punishment!

Neju shifted his position irritably. The sun was setting by now and children passed homewards like birds, sounding their different notes, playing around their elders and drinking at the fountains. The groups thinned. The stragglers passed one by one through the fast emptying park. A little boy of eleven or so with his leg in a brace hitched himself by Neju's bench after everyone else had gone. He had the somber beauty of maimed children: head a little to the side, fragile wrists protruding. Neju stared at him until the child, feeling his gaze, looked his way. The man opened his hand, carelessly revealing a fifty-cent piece, but the boy, with a sad, wise stare, limped on.

9

THE BUS DRIVER from his seat looked down at Mrs. Puchini resignedly; a half-wit, blocking the doorway in the rush hour.

"Come on, lady, I ain't got all night!" He pressed the starter until the engine roared. Perhaps she was sick and couldn't make it up the steps. "Give her a hand there," he called to the man next in line.

Mrs. Puchini was pushed and hauled onto the Sixty-eighth Street crosstown, her mouth still open and her heart thumping behind her great left breast.

"Oh," she cried. "Oh!"

New Yorkers, who are often kind, helped her to a seat and someone even paid her fare, since she was obviously incapable of concentration. She was finding her way home in the way iron is drawn to the magnet: there was no conscious will about her. Now, although Neju's threat and his callous treatment of the image in her likeness had dulled her senses, the woman's real misery lay elsewhere. Certainly, were she not to fulfill his condition, the death sentence was passed, yet Mrs. Puchini *could* fulfill it. Hidden among her few belongings, saved up for years, was the very sum he demanded, even twenty-nine dollars more. Tomorrow she could rise at dawn to bring it to him, but her anguish was not lightened in the least by this solution. The crux of her distress was that Neju was planning to abandon her.

Mrs. Puchini felt Neju's hand laid on her like God's; laid on her body and her soul. She would have done anything he asked of her. Then why did he wish to be rid of her altogether? Did he no longer care to have her under his spiritual control? Was all that anxiety, those stabs of pain in the night, for nothing? She had betrayed her religion and her confessor for another power, and now this power which had labored to possess her was casting her contemptuously aside. She would have liked to have begged him, prayed him not to abandon her, yet, faced with his mockery and coldness, had not dared. Once he received the money, would he soften and take her again into account? No, he would not; he had said he would give her the little doll directly the cash was in his hands, that he would have no use for it further. Dear Christ, what bitter relief had been in his voice!

"Oh!" cried Mrs. Puchini again, pressing her arms against her sides. She had an awful vision of herself tomorrow, wandering through the rain, clutching the waxen doll. How lonely, how unthinkable to be the master of one's own soul.

Mrs. Puchini arrived home late and found her husband and son sitting helpless and hungry in the kitchen. In their abuse and appetite her manner went unnoticed and she made supper mechanically. She even neglected to look at her son's wounded hand about which he had acted so shamefaced. Giovanni was relieved at this. Last night, after he had come home, his mother had seen it immediately. There had been many shrill questions in Italian. Tonight he had expected the same and was nervous and pale. Brown spots had stained the gauze around his wounds and he had not bothered to change the bandage.

It was the evening Mr. Puchini played cards, and he went out as soon as he had eaten, leaving the mother and son together. Then, for the first time that evening, they observed each other with the automatic glance of sympathy which passes between a mother and child once the master is out of the way.

"How's tricks, Ma?" asked Giovanni, and then: "Sit down, can't you? I want to talk to you."

Mrs. Puchini could not bear to speak to anyone, even her son, so, making only a slight sound, she continued washing the dishes. As though all his initiative were drained by her silent refusal, Giovanni sat morosely on in his chair, nursing his bandaged hand. After she had finished her work and swept the floor, Mrs. Puchini passed her son and went into her bedroom, which was the center section of the flat. Giovanni felt the mass of flesh yield to his knee as she pushed by in the narrow space between table and chair. His strength returned. His face hardened and he followed his mother resolutely.

"Ma, I told you I got to talk. Come here." He took her hand and pulled her to a sitting position on the bed. Only then did he notice how limp she was, how flaccid in his grasp. He wondered if she suspected his aims. Mothers often knew things. "Ma," he said, "I want to get married."

With a sort of habitual tenderness she reached out and stroked the black rings of his hair. "How's your hand? Does it still hurt you, *caro mio?*" she asked in Italian.

"Speak English!" he cried, "I can't tell you in Italian. How I hate that goddamn language!"

His nervousness reached her. "Giovanni, what's-a-the matter? So strange you are tonight."

"I got to get married, Ma. You heard me, didn't you?" How was it possible for anyone to be so dense?

"Thats-a-fine, Giovanni. You're a man now." She tried to sound happy but whatever bothered him remained. He sat still a moment, knitting his brows, and then burst out:

"Ma, give me that money you got hid!"

"Money?" she repeated stupidly.

"Yes, Ma, *you* know. Oh, Ma, I got to do things different. She ain't any girl, she's—Christ, I just *got* to have it!" His earnestness, the fresh anguish of his tones, awoke the mother. Here was her child, her last-born son asking her help.

"But, Giovanni, thats-a-all my money—"

"Ma, you don't need it," he cried. "You've got Pa." His selfishness was unconscious and quite pure. He could see no necessity for his mother to have money.

Mrs. Puchini studied her son in silence. It was as though she observed him through her blood rather than through her eyes. Those two dark jellies in her head were blank and their pupils, reaching into her brain, brought forth no message. Yet something spoke, some atavism stronger than magic or terror, because she rose slowly and went to her drawer while Giovanni watched. After much fumbling and unwrapping, she turned and held out to him a quantity of bills tied with a string. He took it.

"Gee, thanks, Ma. I knew you would and I'll pay it back some day, you wait and see. I'll get you a fur coat one of these mornings, and a diamond bracelet too." While he was being effusive, Giovanni secretly longed to escape. His words rang false, even to his own ears.

After she had been left alone, Mrs. Puchini undressed carefully. She folded her wide undergarments on the chair and untied the cheap, badly made corsets that did so little good. Tenderly, almost, she drew off her stockings. There they were, all those sturdy props that had held her up and in for so long. Without them, in her nakedness, she felt like a cripple. Her breasts pulled at her shoulders. The veins on her legs were knotted like fists. Quickly she slipped on her nightgown and got into bed. Her rosary hung above her, wound about the bedpost, and she glanced up at it. She was dazed and tired.

Well, it was for the best. Now she would be in *his* keeping until the last. He would be unable to give her back to herself. She would die, but she would die in his hands. Mrs. Puchini was no philosopher and her wit was limited. Neju had spoken of a power working through him. She could not understand such subtleties. His face, in her mind, was the face of omnipotence. Once again she glanced up at the beads twisted above her head. She must take them and try to pray. She reached up and flicked them loose. Between her calloused fingers they had no feeling and she could not even recall her Hail Mary.

"Full of grace—full of grace—" What did it mean anyway? She felt her soul as calloused and as dry as her fingers.

Then, at once, a sharp pain filled her chest and she caught her breath. So he was thinking of her! He cared enough to torment her. A thrill of joy shook her, followed immediately by fear.

Next morning Mrs. Puchini failed to rise. Her husband and son, scarcely hiding their anxiety and irritation, bent over her at intervals with questions. Once, when Giovanni alone was leaning above her, she whispered:

"Giovanni, I want you to use the money the way you said. Promise your Ma?"

"Why of course," he muttered, resentful that she should speak to him at all on the subject.

She, however, not satisfied, urged again: "On what you said. Remember, Giovanni, on that girl. Not on me."

"On you," he cried, astonished.

"No, *not* on me, on her, to marry like-a-you said."

He noticed then that she had begun to sweat. It was a little past nine and the room was still cold, yet great drops gathered on her face. They formed a dew beneath her eyes. The slight depression of her forehead and the shadowed upper lip shone with moisture. By-and-by the drops rolled sideways and were soaked into her hair. She tore at the blankets and threw them off, and her features were contorted with a bestial terror. She started to scream. Father and son were worse than helpless in the crisis and by the time a doctor arrived Mrs. Puchini was completely delirious. Into her son's ear she poured a babble of sentences that only served to bewilder him further. From time to time she clutched at his sleeve, whimpering:

"Mr. Neju, take-a-me off!" and then, "Don't let me melt, please, Mr. Neju!"

"It's me, Ma! What's the matter, don't you know me? it's Giovanni."

"Giovanni, tell him to take me off!" Then, as if resigning herself, she would sink back gasping, her lips receding as far as the gums and exposing her decayed teeth. In the sparseness of these teeth and in the way they narrowed towards the root, Mrs. Puchini's jaw took on already the appearance of death. Only the thick saliva glittering between the edges of her mouth showed her to be as yet the living and suffering woman.

That Mrs. Puchini was suffering there was no doubt. Her face felt crushed and against the whole front of her body she could feel burning ridges. At times she fancied she was not at home at all, but lying on a rack of fiery metal. She was in miniature and fashioned out of the frail and yielding wax. Drip, drip! her substance rolled over the hot sides of the radiator and fell onto the floor where it hardened into whitish drops. Each drop was torn from her living flesh! Each drop cried Ah! Above, the cold and pitiless face of Neju, enormous as a god's, was cocked her way. Down somewhere, many flights below, the landlady laughed as she stoked the furnace.

Drip, drip.

"Ah!" cried the fat of Mrs. Puchini melting into death.

After a while the dying woman stopped talking altogether. She no longer had the strength to form words other than that rasp which in itself is a kind of speech. Terrible and final address—how well it describes the closing throat, the streak of gall across the heart, yet its language is unknown to the living. At three-thirty an ambulance came and took Mrs. Puchini to the hospital where the Puchinis, father and son, sat stiffly in the waiting room until they were told to go home. Mrs. Puchini did not actually die until after eight in the evening and the only thing astonishing about her death was the enormous amount of weight she had lost recently. The doctors could tell that because her skin was so loose.

"It isn't one of the symptoms. Think she could have been dieting?"

"Well, vanity thy name is woman."

"Women."

"O.K. Speed it up there, son!"

10

GIOVANNI STAYED ALONE in the flat after his father had gone once more to the hospital. It offended him that his mother's clothes were still out, so he put them away. Beneath them he found her worn, imitation-leather purse, a miracle of ugliness which had been even uglier when new. He shook it over the bed. Might as well get all he could, but there was nothing in it save a few coins, an empty change purse and a card. He closed it and sat down again, reading the card idly as it lay beside him on the bed. Again that name: Neju. So his mother went to fortunetellers. Perhaps she had known then that she was to die.

He lifted his head and called out: "Ma! Ma!" It was really on his sorrow that he was calling; it was impossible for him to feel his loss. It was like being told after a heavy meal that there was no food left in the world, that he would never eat again. Later, when he had fasted long enough, there would be time to crave for that maternal bread. Yet the echo of his call and the appalling void of a house where the fire is out made Giovanni jump to his feet. He went quickly to his room and took out a suit of clothes from the closet. They were brand new, a present from Charles, and he wore them now for the first time, because tonight he had been asked to No. 5. Until now Giovanni had known only the other house, the gloomy No. 7, bound so strangely to its rich neighbor. The new suit, although expensive, became him less than the clothes he quitted. The round forms of his muscles were smoothed over so that there was almost a pudgy look to him and all his Latin poetry was dimmed. Never mind, he was proud of it. He crammed his five hundred dollars—sum of death—into his wallet and, leaving the flat, walked swiftly across town.

A New York sleet fell upon the pavements, white in the lamp light, muddy and dark beneath his feet. He shivered with cold; he had not wished to wear his old topcoat and, for fear of deforming his new trousers, refrained from putting his hands in the pockets.

Giovanni, stepping hurriedly through the sleet in his new suit, was on his way to a party and was quite unconscious that it was an unusual or callous thing to do: either Charles' world was as yet too separate from Giovanni's in its joys and sorrows, or else, as with many people after a loss, he simply did the next thing scheduled in his brain. He could not even speculate on what his evening would be like and had really no idea of the society into which he would shortly be plunged. Names well known in the international set would be there. Wealth would be there too, although less of it than one might suppose if one were looking in at the window The little court of Charles, the Duke of Sixty-fifth Street! The Pere Laborde, bent on self-deception; Sheila, her voice scraping the air; a movie star (second-rate); a dancer, (first-rate); a prince or two. Giovanni would surely learn the language in no time and was bound to be a success with his male freshness. He would enjoy flattery, no doubt, and grow to expect it, to coax it out of both sexes, to need it. He would learn, in other words, to be kept.

Giovanni this first time did not dare ring the bell of No. 5 but used his own key to the house next door. The sewers still spoke in the street outside, telling their story of corruption and fetid decay. He was glad to be quit of them and to be going through the double door until now unknown to him. He meant to follow the sound of revelry to the guests below, and, indeed, hearing their voices as soon as he entered Charles' room, he had no difficulty making his way to the front stairs. There he almost fell over Candy, who was sitting on the first step with her knees up to her chin.

"Candy!" he cried.

But she did not say anything, only putting her finger to her lips with a little smile as children do who are afraid of being heard and sent to bed. How untouchable and remote she seemed to the man who had possessed her so short a time ago. In an instant he realized the stupidity of his thoughts of marriage. A tremor passed through him. Some desire, either to hurt her or to lighten his animal unease, made him draw out his wallet and thrust the wad of bills into Candy's lap.

"There," he said. "There!" And was astonished to hear his voice so harsh.

Candy covered the money with her hands and looked up at him, startled. He passed her quickly and disappeared into the well of talk and laughter below.

As Giovanni entered the long, narrow salon which occupied a whole floor of Charles' house, he looked around him warily but unafraid. There were thirty-odd people in the room, and what struck the eye at once was that the men, as a whole, were younger than the women. Rather, they had a boyish air about them corresponding to the blond girlishness of women in another day. On coming closer, one saw that the youth was an effect rather than a fact. Giovanni did not feel sure of these people at all, but, choosing the most glittering of the women, went up to her at once. It was Leonine.

Leonine was an old friend of the Duke's and was ten years his senior. It was due to Leonine that Charles had met his rich wife and Leonine had remained through the seasons the chief jewel of his social entourage. She drew an elegance behind her from year to year, like a shawl of such quality that it outlasts a lifetime. Leonine's hair was of that dull, silvery blond which famous coiffeurs try in vain to copy and which age must fight to tarnish. Her eyes, in contrast, were still brown and hot. Her walk, a mixture of hair and eyes, was so highbred, so superbly easy as to appear at times almost vulgar. She moved from her thigh bones and there was a brutal beauty in the fold and clip of those high-jointed limbs.

Giovanni now confronted this woman with a boldness and self-confidence that cannot be derived from manners. Scenting the original aroma of the woman, which clung to her despite her age, he became at once a man, any man, a male, master of the world.

"I am sure you are Giovanni," she said immediately. "Charles has spoken so much of you and your talent."

"Talent?" Giovanni was naively taken off guard.

"Come now," said Leonine, narrowing her eyes—innocent naivete displeased her, "Charles only likes young men with talent."

Giovanni, taking her words as they were meant, flushed a dark, congested red. "Shall I show *you* my talent then?" he asked with a coarse intonation, half making a movement of both hands which she could not fail to comprehend. He recognized suddenly, in one of those clear flashes of the brain,' that Leonine's insinuation was an echo of Candy's when she had come to his roam, and that his reply was only a parody of what he had then been able to answer.

But Leonine was delighted with it and not at all offended. "My dear," she murmured, "you must calm down. Remember, I am a friend of Charles'." She adjusted the strap of her shoulder with that insolence of youth which is intoxicating when it occurs in an older woman. The passage had amused her although she would not for the world have trespassed on Charles' property. The Duke was too important in her life. He paid her an allowance and wore her like a pearl. A pearl *needs* to be worn. She often quarrelled with him nonetheless, for he was intensely jealous when she appeared at any big house or salon other than his. At this moment she was contemplating being unfaithful to Charles in this respect on the following night, and the knowledge gave her extra nonchalance.

Sheila drifted into the room. She had been upstairs trying to force Charles to come up after her, but she had failed and now she saw the reason: he was not there himself. An uncontrollable aggravation made her flutter her hands. She was dressed in a chiffon evening dress which tied at the throat. Her long sleeves showed the sickly white of her arms through the stuff and her hair thrust unbecoming curls around her face.

'Of course,' thought Leonine, 'she should never have grown out of her school uniform. A white blouse, a jumper, and hair brushed back are the only things that could ever make her look clean—and patent leather pumps on Sunday.'

Leonine herself always found someone who would dress her for nothing, and was clad this time in slipper satin of a rich brown color which heightened her jungle grace.

"Good evening, Sheila dear," said Leonine.

"Good evening," said Sheila. Her voice, from lack of range, could hide none of the hatred and jealousy she felt for the other woman, and neither could she help asking: "Where's Charles?"

Leonine shrugged. "Oh, I suppose he went to see the little Rollo dance. It's his opening. Charles pestered me all morning to come, but really it's too hot and crowded there and it will be better to hear your husband describe it later."

Sheila turned her eyes vaguely onto Giovanni. He had not seen her since his first day at No. 7, and he was puzzled as to her place in the household. Had Charles' wife been Leonine, he could have understood it better.

"I've seen you somewhere, haven't I?" asked Sheila. She studied him without hope—a nice enough looking boy, but Charles' friend, not hers. They never were hers. They all looked at her in the same way: coldly, as though she were a piece of furniture that they accepted as guests must. Privately they thought her unsuitable.

"Good evening, Mmm," said Giovanni.

"Her name's not Mmm, it's *Madame La Duchesse* if you want to be continental, and Sheila if you have permission," Leonine said in a voice between coaxing, flirtation and insolence, but Giovanni took the lesson with a natural suppleness.

"Good evening, *Madame la Duchesse,*" he corrected himself, and grinned at Leonine.

"You are charming," she said, "and you may bring me some champagne."

Giovanni went to get it and brought two glasses, offering one to Sheila.

"No thanks," said Sheila. "I hate it, really."

Giovanni drank it himself, looking at Leonine over the rim of his glass. At this moment a rather pudgy youth came up to them and put out the tip of his tongue at Leonine by way of greeting. He was, in fact, Leonine's lover, or passed as such.

"Sheila," murmured Leonine, "you have met Mr. Rogers, haven't you?"

Mr. Rogers extended one of his smooth, moist hands which Sheila just touched.

"Giovanni, do tell me your last name," begged Leonine, showing her smile.

"Puchini."

"Ah, yes. Mr. Puchini, Mr. Rogers." Again the hand was extended, but as Giovanni took it he was astonished to find the middle finger bent against his palm. He let go quickly.

"Are you a New Yorker?" asked Mr. Rogers languidly, lifting his head—a mistaken trick of his, for it was at once apparent that the point of his chin and the base of his throat were connected like a dowager's.

"Sure," answered Giovanni.

"I was just asking as I didn't think I'd seen you. I do adore to meet new people, don't you? Leoni, don't you think he'd be perfect for Skitri?"

Skitri was a painter in fashion.

"Giovanni's very occupied," said Leonine. "Isn't he, *ma chere?"* This to Sheila.

"Well I really don't know much about him," answered Sheila in her absurd voice, and the other three scorned her down to her very bones.

"Come, Leoni sweet," coaxed Mr. Rogers, "I want to have you meet Laras, the Persian I told you about. He has the most fabulous collection of embroidered silks. I must take you there one day."

They moved off and as they did so one could see that the man's dinner jacket had a pink lining. It was quite apparent when Mr. Rogers pirouetted on Leonine's arm. Leonine's brown satin slid over her reins and polished the shifting mounds of her rump.

"She is old but attractive," said Giovanni, pointing his thumb in the direction of the departing woman.

"Well, everyone grows old," said Sheila, refusing in her usual way to take the comfort offered.

This was such a novel idea to Giovanni that he stared. Sheila said: "You seem to have hurt your hand," but the words were uttered with such indifference that there was no reply to make. Giovanni looked around him and saw that Pere Laborde was entering the salon. The priest was sallow and agitated from meeting Candy on the stairs, and his yellowish robes matched his skin under the electric light. He was immediately surrounded, however, by women who wanted to talk French and to whom the idea of a private priest was exotic. Here was another gem in the Duke's collection.

Pere Laborde was telling about a young Canadian girl who had entered a severe religious order. Her parents had begged him to intervene and he was describing the scene. "There she was," he said in French, "looking through the grille with the most charming air in the world. How could I rob the Church of such a delightful flower. Her veil became her better than the choicest hat in Paris!" And in his mind he pictured Candy, safe forever behind a grille with the veil covering that questioning brow, that sudden Indian curve. How happily he would smile at her then! With what heavenly forgiveness! No jealousy would mar their intercourse, no uncouth gesture from his frustrate heart would make her wince. She would be saved everlastingly from womanhood, from the void of woman which must be filled by man. No more could she sit on the stairs and make her knees sharp beneath her skirt and yearn towards the world.

His listeners, too, felt charmed by his words. There they were, young and pure, brides of Christ, being admired by holy men with a touch of innocent roguishness.

In a cloud of chatter Charles burst into the room accompanied by a very ugly, half-drunk woman and a blond youth.

"Shit, I tell you!" he cried loudly. "Excuse me that I must say that word, but it is the only one to describe the performance we have just seen. I told Rollo. He wept but I was firm. I said to him: 'My dear, one does that in the water closet, not on the stage!'" Charles spoke in high, excited tones and his choice of words was a deliberate eccentricity which was encouraged by laughter from every part of the room. Pere Laborde snickered behind his hand and Giovanni, finding it genuinely funny, gave a great guffaw. Think of speaking about such things among such guests! The Duke must really be a very important man.

Only Sheila did not smile and now could not decide which was worse: having him go out and enjoy himself without her, or seeing the success he had in which she occupied no place. The laughter of their guests would never be raised at any word she could utter and, in any case, she was incapable of conversation. Her nerves fretted the thread of her talk until it broke. Standing unsmiling and plain amidst this general laughter, Sheila felt a dull agony well up inside her. Looking around with her small, dimmed glance, she got the feeling that all these guests, these toadies of her husband's, were not laughing at what he said at all, but at her, their hostess. It was as if they all knew a secret of which she was ignorant. And there was contempt mingled with the laughter. They seemed to say: "Coward. You could easily know it if you wished. You are afraid. You don't dare know. You prefer your whining and self-deceit."

Examining all their pitiless faces, Sheila turned around aimlessly on her long shoes. How could one pity such a creature?

It was at this moment that Neju was ushered into the room by the butler. Charles, who happened to be facing that way, saw him at once and focussed his eyes by drawing up the slack muscles of his cheeks.

"It can't be, can it?" he cried. "It can't be Nigel?"

"Carlos, Charles!" Nigel's voice cracked with relief at the tone of the Duke's greeting.

"So I was right! Nigel, you are the one person in the world I wanted!" Charles ran forward, fell on the charlatan's neck and kissed him. "Ah, *mon cher,"* he continued, "why did you not come to see me before? What have you been doing?"

Nigel, or Neju, moved smartly forward to salute his hostess. With hard eyes he saw, as he took her hand, that she was of no account in the house, and he admired Charles from the depth of his heart. "Madame," he said, "you see I have availed myself of your kind invitation."

Sheila felt his cold, brittle hand touch hers. She hated it. 'If only once in every month, in every year, Charles would kiss *me* on the cheeks with so much joy,' she thought, yet she was wrong. Had her husband done so, she would have repulsed him. It was not kisses on her cheeks that Sheila wanted, and perhaps she was too far gone for any kisses. Desire turned in upon itself creates, they say, a salad for which there is no dressing. Sheila went quickly from the salon and up the stairs.

Candy still sat there.

"Go to bed," said Sheila. I don't like you to sit there on the stairs like that. You are not a child."

"Yes, I suppose I am too old for a child's privileges," agreed Candy, rising: "But Mama, when shall I have others?"

"I don't think you'll ever have them," said the little bird voice of Sheila. "There aren't any, you know."

"In that case, good night, Mama dear," said Candy.

11

* *Candy's diary:*

.... My diary, I have neglected you, have I not? It is a week since I wrote and I see that I asked you far too many questions that time. How stupid of me to ask you anything! What if you should answer me? Oh, I shall flatter you, lie to you and drip tears on top of wet ink, but I hope you will never, never answer me. Enough! Let us speak of the weather. It is dull, but all the ice has melted and the workers in the construction outside have built a little house in the middle of the street. Is it to keep tools in, I wonder, or have they just made it so that they can run in and have a drink of wine?

He drinks wine. I smelt it on his breath that time. Ah diary, you would like to know about that, wouldn't you?

You would like me to speak of my experience: How I Became a Woman, or better, How I Became a Fallen Woman. Last time I wrote I was all fantasy, dreaming of specters in a garden! Now let us stick to facts. First, I have a lot of money. Not the money I am always told I have, yet which only exists in the minds of parents, bankers, and trustees. No, not that kind at all. *This* money is real. I keep it hidden where no one will find it. It was given me by someone. I was sitting on the stairs listening to some quite instructive conversations between Papa's guests when this someone came by and put it in my lap. This someone lives in No. 7 now. There is another newcomer to the house next door as well; an older man with white hair who is being Papa's Hope of the Future. It seems he makes dolls and Papa is going to start a puppet theatre with him and have plays written for it by all the famous authors. The dolls are, besides, to be portraits of real people in wax, so enemies can be made into villains and friends into heroes. Papa is in ecstasies, as one can imagine. So is Pere Laborde, who is planning to produce a miracle play. For my part, I am taking lessons in modeling with Nigel (that's the creature's name) and find it quite bearable. I take them in No. 7.

I have seen no one of importance since the money episode, although I sometimes think I hear his steps when I go for my lessons.......

* * *

Candy stopped writing. She would not have admitted it for the world but she lived and breathed in the rhythm of Giovanni's life. Informed of his comings and goings, through means known to lonely young girls for whom listening is unavoidable, her heart moved towards him like tides towards the moon. The whole femininity, the whole flow of her blood, was turned his way. Human beings, it is said, have a salt base to their chemical makeups. They are, by heritance, creatures of the ocean. The sea flows between matter and spirit. Thus the tides shift in their beings with the moon's wax and wane. The spring floods trace corrosive marks upon their senses. Eclipses convulse their hearts. Candy was at that time in a woman's life when she most feels these mysteries. She fancied a constant tugging in her breast, as when the sea sucks and pulls at the shore, and sometimes at night she awoke to hear her pulses pound against the sheets, a rhythmic rustling in arteries and veins. Then, without actually thinking, she would feel these new impulses turn towards her lover. Everything became one with him: the darkness of her room became his darkness; the night air, his breath; her own flesh seemed actually his. At such times a sort of fear came over her that she could so easily lose her identity. She would grit her teeth and say: "I am Candy. Candy!" Then she would go back to sleep, pressing herself down against the bed.

On that morning when she had finished writing in her diary, she spent a few minutes with Josie before going to her modeling lesson. Josie was tidying her young mistress' closet and taking out those clothes which had grown too small for her. The servant was careful and meticulous and, having finished with the closet, went on to the chest of drawers to see what needed mending.

Candy said: "Josie, you sleep upstairs at the back of the other house, don't you?"

"Why of course, Miss Candy, you know that very well."

"Do you see the others?"

"Others, Miss Candy? I don't have time to see anyone. I just go about my business."

"Josie, you know the man with white hair who gives me lessons at present; he lives below you. Did you know?"

"Does he, Miss Candy?"

"Yes, you perfidious creature, and there is another man who lives right up on top, on the same floor as you, but in front. I mean a new one. I know the old one left, the one who taught me music."

"Well, I daresay," said Josie, closing the top drawer and getting on to the next, and then: "Miss Candy, you have no call to ask me all these questions. Why not leave me to work, like a good girl?"

"A good girl," chanted Candy. "How nice those words sound! Just for that I shall put a ribbon on my hair." She went to her mirror and tied a thin, scarlet ribbon around the mane of hair which was drawn back behind her ears. Against the simplicity of her costume, this coquetry was as noticeable as a new dress would have been on another.

"I can't understand it," said Josie more to herself than otherwise, "you are missing a whole set of new underwear."

Candy thought of the stained rags she had once pressed between her thighs. "Ah Josie," she cried, "whatever is to become of me?" Without waiting for an answer, she left the room and started downstairs to her lessons. She passed through her father's room and watched him a moment as he lay asleep.

Charles was a person whose intimate morning life was lived as publicly as that of an old-time king. There were three doors to his bedroom: one, into the study, through which Candy had come; one into his wife's bedroom; and, of course, the double door into No. 7. Sheila hardly ever used her door and it was the only one which was closed now. Charles' secretary, a nervous man with strained eyes, was already answering telephone calls and coming in every few minutes to see if Charles were awake. He was there at this instant, standing uncertainly near the bed, and he gave Candy a harried bow.

She came nearer to observe this sleeping man of whom she knew at once too little and too much. His eyelids bombed out over the protruding eyes. She could trace the iris through them, round, moving disks beneath the stretched lids. One of his hands lay on the sheet and, with the soft gesture of slumber, he passed it up and over his face. Soon he would wake. Candy passed into the other house.

Nigel's room was situated on the same floor as the Duke's bedroom in No. S. One simply went down the hall of No. 7 and it was there at the head of the stairs. Nigel had a room, a bath, and a telephone and had already grown quite accustomed to his good luck.

Of course, after Mrs. Puchini's failure to turn up with the five hundred dollars, Nigel had been thoroughly annoyed. He had been so sure that she was in the palm of his hand! He had waited all day, roving from one end of the room to the other and casting angry looks at the wax doll as it lay on the chair. Towards evening he had known there was no use in waiting further and in desperation had decided to go to Charles' anyway. It had worked perfectly. Charles had taken him upstairs to his room, and there they had talked for a long time of the old days, bringing back hours when they had both been young and free.

"But now, you Charles, you are rich and happy. You have recovered your titles"—a polite way of saying it—"while I am still completely unknown."

"Ah, *mon cher!*" The Duke's voice was melancholic. "To be rich is not all. If you knew how tedious are most of my days! I have no real friends. Everyone of them wants something from me. If it weren't for my money and my house not one would come and see me. My dear, I must buy now what others used to buy from me."

"But your wife, your daughter, I have heard you have a very beautiful daughter, and your wife is charming."

Charles jumped to his feet and clasped his hands together. He pressed them against his breast. "My wife!" he cried. "She torments me! Every day there are tears and scenes. You will see, she will be angry that we have stayed here together talking of when we were young. Poof, I don't care! Tell me about yourself. I will help you, Nigel. I am so bored with my life." And he took a benzedrine tablet from a little china box which was shaped like a heart.

It was in talking that they hit upon the scheme of having a puppet theatre. Charles felt the need of a new interest to attract the intelligentsia and the artists and this idea seemed to him both novel and amusing. Nigel would live in No. 7, where he would work on his dolls. They were to be likenesses of people in society, of that harried set that circles Europe and America between wars. It was a heaven-sent chance for gossip, blackmail, and reward. They would do the classics, and modern playwrights would vie with each other to serve them. Well-known designers would beg to do their costumes and scenery. Charles was like a child in his enthusiasm.

By now, a week later, Nigel had made several new dolls and had kept the best of his old ones. In the afternoons and evenings he observed the people in the salon, studied his victims. In the morning he gave lessons to Candy, who was completely without talent. Charles had had Giovanni make Nigel a huge worktable, six boards laid on saw horses, and his room, which gave on the backyard, was filled with a grey light untouched by sun.

Nigel did not much care for Candy and, as she came in to her lesson this morning, he noted the ribbon with displeasure. Giovanni, whom he had asked to pose earlier, was still there, sitting by the window. He was not looking as well as he had. His hair, a little long, gave the impression it must soil his collar. There was a large ring on his finger, this and the watch on his wrist, along with too much praise from the wrong people, had set a complacent touch at the corners of his lips. Soon they would be sulky. When he saw Candy, he made a convulsive movement and it was obvious that he had been told women must be greeted standing. In the end, however, he could not bear to rise and remained in the same position: his strong legs apart and his hands spread on his knees.

"Am I disturbing you?" Candy asked.

"Not at all. I was just finishing, and while I do so you can work on your own and use the same model—or are you tired, Giovanni?"

"Yeah, I guess I feel tired," said Giovanni. "I feel kind of cramped from sitting still." He got up and came over to the big table where Candy had already started working. They were both intensely aware of one another, but only Candy was really suffering. In the presence of a female, even the beloved, Giovanni was still a cock. Candy, who had flushed at first, was now pale. Her head was bent over her modeling. Her fingers worked in and out of the wax without promise. When Giovanni came up behind her, she could hardly repress a shudder. He reached over her shoulder and fingered one of the wax figures.

"That looks—looked—sort of like my Ma," he said.

"Yes?" asked Nigel carelessly. "It was made from an Italian woman."

"I guess my Ma had too many children," said Giovanni. "I'm not gonna let *my* wife do that. She's gonna keep *her* shape." He looked down as he spoke, at Candy's narrow shoulders.

Nigel was astonished. He had not realized that Giovanni, whom he still hardly knew, was so naive. Didn't he realize what poor taste he was showing? 'Really,' Nigel thought, 'Charles plays a dangerous game to take in such a raw recruit.' He said aloud, dryly: "It depends on what shape they have in the beginning, but I hope, my poor boy, you are not thinking of anything so unrewarding as marriage." He restated it with emphasis: "So *banal* as marriage."

Giovanni was easily wilted by this mature point of view. "Who? Me?" he said, blushing and trying to laugh. Then, to cover his embarrassment, he took up the little figure from the table and turned it over. Stuck to its feet was a white calling card with red and black lettering and he stared at it for a few moments. "I guess I'll go now," he said abruptly.

In leaving, Giovanni brushed past Candy's chair deliberately. She could feel his warmth against her shoulders.

12

GIOVANNI STARED AT Neju's card. He had closed the door softly and could hear behind it a quiet murmur: Candy, no doubt, asking a question of her teacher. Down the hall he saw the open door between the houses and he knew that by now Charles would be waking up. Giovanni wanted to think, but in the gloomy passage he felt like a trapped animal to whom only instinct is left. He could not bear to go to his room on the top floor, so he went down the stairs, hoping to escape without meeting anyone. Yet there Pere Laborde stood silently, his robe gleaming in the shadows. The priest had one hand on the knob of his own door and the other was gathering his skirts with a womanish movement. His face was yellow and lined. He was consumed with jealousy of Nigel. Every morning since the day Candy had started taking lessons in wax modeling, Pere Laborde had done nothing but bite his lips and try to control the bile which poured into his blood.

Giovanni stopped short at the sight of him. This mysterious Dominican was, as yet, someone with whom he had no idea of how to act. If he were a real churchman, what was he doing in this house? How angry a priest should be at all the happenings and at every personage. How severely

Giovanni would be held up to the piercing light of God. Yet Pere Laborde did not look at all stern. There was a furtiveness about him, and when they met on the stairs or in the salon of No. 5, his priestly greeting was nervous and there was a half-smile on his lips.

Now Pere Laborde was startled by the sight of the youth, whom he had not known to be in Nigel's room. "Ah, *mon fils,* good morning! It seems we are fated always to meet on the stairs." He giggled, or rather snickered, sadly and without meaning. As Giovanni made no reply and avoided his eyes, he continued: "I realize we do not see much of each other even though we do live in the same house, but I know all about you."

At this Giovanni gave a start and looked up at him beneath the fringe of his lashes. Pere Laborde went on quickly: "Yes I know, I have heard very fine things about you, from your dear patron, *ce cher Charles.* What a good man he is! You must be—and you are, I am sure—grateful for such opportunities to get on in the world." Then as he saw the boy shuffling his feet, he said, "You are in a hurry and I won't keep you now, but remember—I am a priest. If you have any troubles or if anything should bother you, do not hesitate to come to me."

Giovanni muttered something incomprehensible and retreated out the front door. His trials were not yet over. He had still to pass his old companions on the construction. At first he had greeted them in a half shy, half swaggering manner. Now there was silence on both sides, and as he passed he could feel their eyes upon him: eyes whose expressions he did not dare read. The very depths of their surprise and incredulity held them silent—even Mike, who had been his close friend. Mike's eyes, of that pale, pointed, New York grey, were on him now and he must cross their shafts directly. Giovanni sensed his friend there in his path and clenched his fists in his pockets. They could have touched. Giovanni hunched his shoulders and turned away his face. He heard a soft voice say:

"Gettin' to need a haircut, aintcha?"

He pretended not to have heard, but when he turned the corner and looked again at Neju's card it was limp with his palm's sweat.

"He's just jealous," he muttered to himself. "They're all jealous because I don't have to work no—anymore."

All the same, a pang of tenderness for Mike stabbed at his heart. He could hardly recall the time he had not known Mike, and now they would never be together again. Aside from an averted face, a low and bitter phrase, no further words would pass between them. Tears rose to Giovanni's eyes and in his imagination, boylike, he pictured situations that would leave Mike irrevocably in his debt.

Giovanni walked several blocks immersed in such reveries, his face expressing every stage of his imaginary heroism. He began to feel better and threw out his chest. The litheness came back into his stride. He turned into the park, since his destination was on its far side. The trees were swelling into that thick outline which betokens the approach of spring, but the wind was strong and smelt of snow. Giovanni sniffed the air like a stallion and paced with limber feet on the muddy paths. His ungloved hands swung beside his thighs, the palms turned slightly to the front as is the habit with manual workers; the blood swelling and pouring into the big veins of his left forearm made the freshly healed cuts ache. He soon lifted up the hand which had been mutilated and nursed it close to his chest, blowing on it for warmth.

In the park he shook himself free of the Giovanni who wanted a life of ease, or rather who had stumbled blindly into that want, simply out of accident, because Charles had noticed him on the street. Oh, Giovanni remembered the beginning clearly. He had been sitting for an instant on the steps of No. 7, fixing the zipper on his jacket. Out of the corner of his eye he had seen Charles, a small man dressed in black, hovering near, and finally, just as he had the zipper in its groove once more, the man had come up and said:

"Excuse me, but do you know anything about plumbing? You see, I've lost the cross I wear around my neck. It went down the washstand sink. The chain broke. It was my mother's."

Giovanni, with his inborn helpfulness and geniality, had consented to try to help. "You probably need a real plumber though, Mister."

"No, no, I have an instinct about people. Your face looks sympathetic. I knew you would help me." Although these words were said in a loud, almost comic voice, the rich man's great spoiled eyes were laid upon Giovanni like a disease and it was impossible not to understand them. After a silence, Charles continued: "It is because I have so much money that I am so lonely."

The Duke's accent had lent a certain pathetic appeal to his proposal, to this verbal contract whose terms were never stated but which were, nonetheless, understood and signed between them both.

Now, a fortnight later, Giovanni, nursing and blowing on his hand, studied the ring which had been given him by his patron. It was one of those stones that are pressed together out of the dust of jewels—emeralds, in this case—and it had neither the defiant flaws of the precious stone nor the sweet clarity of a semiprecious one. The best that could be said for it was that it was large and anyone could see it; also that more money had been paid for it than it was worth. This, too, might lend it glamour in some eyes. Charles had given the ring in repentance for his act of brutality and Giovanni thought it very fine—and his watch too, of course.

Then, in his other hand, Giovanni felt again the piece of pasteboard that had driven him out of the house. All other reflections and ideas vanished from his mind. Neju's card had had on Giovanni a peculiar effect. On reading it in Nigel's room, he had felt something turn over in the depths of his consciousness. He had heard his mother say that name as she was rocked to death in her delirium. He had seen it duplicated among her things and now, sticking to the little image which so resembled her, it had literally lifted him out into the street. He could not as yet connect his mother's words, the card, or the waxen doll into any kind of sequence, and he did not even conceive that Neju and the Nigel who seemed so unpleasant and cold were the same person. Simply, like an animal to whom a trail has been made plain, he followed Neju's spoor across the park.

The first flakes of snow began to drift down from the sky, blown sideways by the wind. Far more beautiful jewels than the kept are ever given sprinkled Giovanni's hair. He arrived at his destination.

"He don't live here any more," said the landlady, and was about to close the door when she saw the snow shining on his hair and lashes. Her shoebutton eyes softened. "Come in, young feller. I'll see if he left an address." She knew that this was not the case but she pretended to search among some papers on an old table.

"He went away with a big car, chauffeur and all. I guess someone died and left him a fortune. Someone he killed off most likely, with *his* peculiar goings on!"

"Goings on?" Giovanni half whispered it. He did not want to know any more, yet the words were drawn out of his body.

"Sure, goings on! He used to make people's pictures out of wax and then whatever he did to the pictures would happen to them, see? Especially if he needed dough! Served 'em right, silly cows to come running into strange pastures.

Some of them acted like they was in love with him. Him! Can you imagine? Fish eyes, egg face, and all. Why there was one woman, a big, fat wop—no offence," she added hastily, "we're all Americans here."

Her visitor's attitude, however, pulled her up short. He was wearing such an unnatural, strained grimace that she grew suspicious. "Say, what are you so curious about? What was this Neju to you anyway?" Her face had grown as spiteful as though he had repulsed her.

Giovanni had heard enough and was out before she could manage to insult him. He was dazed. Against his will the pieces of a cruel story were fitting themselves together relentlessly in his mind. He had the impression that once it was complete and all the pieces joined, his life would fall apart in their stead. The image of his mother's poor little room on the East *Side* and of her intimate clothes lying so neatly on the chair rose before his eyes. How meekly she had lain down that final night! How meekly she had given up to him her worldly treasure! She had been grotesque in her flesh, stupid in her mind, and she had, indeed, wandered into strange pastures. Yet Giovanni himself, had he not so wandered? Where had he put those petty savings of day by day? 'Oh, Candy, what use are savings to you and me?' And the man who was somehow responsible, where was he now? With a trumped-up name, he was drinking cream and eating fat in the Duke's house!

Giovanni gave a cry of rage. He could hardly see in front of him and there came to him a sudden longing to forget, to drug his mind for a little while. He turned into a bar, ordered a bourbon and drank it at a gulp. Almost at once a comforting warmth went down the center of his being, like a column. He ordered another.

The barman brought the bottle along. "I've got it to sell," he said. "If you can pay up, I can pour it out."

"Here," said Giovanni. He took off his watch and ring and threw them on the bar. "Tell me when that's used up," he said, and when his glass was refilled tossed it down neat. He relaxed and looked around him. Although it was nearly in the afternoon, there were several men already collected about the chipped, moist bar. The man next to him ordered a beer and Giovanni offered him a whiskey. As the bar filled, he stood many more rounds and felt himself among friends. The talk was of liquor, sex, the ring and racing. The barman leaned confidingly towards his customers and told his experiences. After a time, when everyone was mellow, life itself was discussed, tenderly, remotely, without bitterness or rancour. Giovanni's hair, curling from melted snow, spiralled down to his eyes, and he raked it back to show a forehead knotted with the effort of philosophy.

Then the inevitable happened: a woman came in. The talk was shattered like a crystal. All were silent, watching this strange beast in their cage. All were uneasy and hostile to those twitching skirts. The woman was a tart, not really a professional whore, but not just a wild girl, either. She was very young, with a round shiny nose and a body shaped from the side like an S. She sat down at a table first, then leapt up and put a nickel in the juke box. She went back to her seat in ugly jerks that were meant to represent the rhythm of dance steps. Her face, over adolescent pimples, was covered with a sort of reddish paste, and she constantly re-powdered her stifled skin for fear men would think her diseased. Over her thin and still childish lips she had pointed two curving arcs which came almost up to her nostrils. They were dark and greasy and she was careful never to smile. Her small jaws, however, worked and reworked her gum.

The men decided to ignore her but she could not do the same for them. She crossed her knees, crossed them the other way, got up time and again to look at the juke box and twitched at her shoulder straps inside her blouse. Every man there knew he could have her and all any of them wanted was to talk as before.

Other women, and some couples, came in. The atmosphere changed. The group at the bar dissolved, leaving Giovanni standing there like the stone of a peach which no one eats. His mellowness left him and a sudden fear of being alone took him. Over his future grave a hawk flew. Its dark wings sent a chill along his spine. He waited until the tart got up again and then he took his foot from the bar rail, wheeled and confronted her in a stride. With a gesture that was more of anguish than of lust, he thrust his clenched fist between her legs. She stood quite still. Giovanni's hand was stretched out of his sleeve and he could feel against his naked wrist the jerk and throb of her crotch. The tight skirt, which his action had made even tighter, forced into outline the meanness of her hip, the flatness of her behind with its sagging edges.

"You look like a good kid," he said.

Her face was impassive, her jaws still worried the gum. She nodded towards the bartender. "Joe there's got a room he lets me use—if I pay him."

Giovanni withdrew his arm reluctantly. He would have liked to stay there in the bar all night with her in front of him.

The matter was arranged and he found himself in a little room with the tart pressed up against him. She remained fully clothed (she thought it immodest to undress) and the long afternoon's drinking had left Giovanni limp. He took her into his arms, nonetheless, and began to kiss her throat. She stiffened. Perhaps she thought he had drunk too much, or sensed a torment in him that she did not want to share—or, who knows, something else in his manner, some new thing, might have put her off. She backed away.

"Why, you're no good at all," she said in a voice of childish fury. "I bet you haven't even got it to give! And you put your arm like that and all! Cheater, that's what you are. A real cheat!"

She flounced out of the room so fast he did not have time to answer. In a few minutes he followed with hanging head and unsteady gait. The barman tossed the ring on the bar as Giovanni passed through.

"Can't use it son, it ain't real. Say, why don't you make them give you real jewelry?" Despite these words he sounded sorry for Giovanni, but he was careful to keep the watch.

Out on the street Giovanni began to cry. It was dark by now and the snow was falling thickly. His feet sank in the soft white carpet and all city sounds were muted. Only his tears sounded clearly to him. They welled out of his heart like a waterfall. He felt himself the victim of a hundred desires, sucked as by vampires for his juicy youth. And they were all laughing now! Charles was joking with his guests and planning his evening. The tart was mocking him at the bar. Candy was smiling into her mirror as she brushed her hair, and Nigel, who was Neju, had in some way destroyed his mother. What was Giovanni to do about that?

One thing certain, he must go back to that house. They had him in their net. He stumbled along, weeping.

This time Giovanni had no need to cross the park, he was too far downtown, and he skirted it on Fifty-ninth Street, walking close up against its walls. Now and then, when a branch overhanging the sidewalk dumped its burden of moist snow on him, he shook himself and hunched his shoulders brutishly. There were few people out, and those there were hurried along on the opposite pavement. Only a solitary child, a little girl of about seven, noticed him. She had a hoop in her bare hands which was almost larger than she: a thin, shiny circle of wood. As Giovanni passed under a lamp she confronted him and it was as though she had come out of the park trees, like a dryad. He stopped. He could find strength neither to pass around her nor to push her aside. She looked up at him dispassionately.

"You're crying," she said.

"So what?" he muttered shamefully and angrily.

"Grownups don't cry," she stated, and as he had no answer to that, she held the great hoop out in front of her body like a frame. Inside its curve she swayed from side to side and repeated: "They don't cry! They don't! They don't!" Her voice was a sing-song, cruel and sweet.

Suddenly she tired and with an impudent movement ran off along the snowy and deserted pavement, rolling her hoop. Once it fell, but she managed by the way she picked it up to prove to the world that she had wanted the hoop to fall, that it had been a difficult feat to manage exactly there and then. She was triumphant and flicked the white triangle of her face back at Giovanni. He was no longer watching. At her words he had felt a strange weight added to his sorrow. He, too, had believed that grownups never cried.—How short a time ago that had been, and when had the child left him, soul and sinew, and the man come in, the man that wept?

At last Giovanni arrived at No. 7 and mounted the stairs slowly and clumsily, holding on to the banister. Pere Laborde, coming through from dinner in No. 5, saw him.

"My son," said the priest. Giovanni stopped in front of Nigel's room and raised his reddened eyes.

"What is it, Giovanni, are you in trouble?" He moved towards the boy and Giovanni gave a convulsive sob.

"Father, look at this." In an instant he had opened Nigel's door and turned on the light. With a lunge he picked up the waxen Mrs. Puchini and held the image out for the priest to see. "The bastard. The dirty bastard. I'll show him how to make dolls!" He took up a hammer which had been used to nail the worktable together. Half blindly he started to crush the figures that were lying there. Again and again he struck, holding his mother's image in his free hand. He panted with exertion, and his drunkenness churned inside of him. He threw the hammer down and was sick among the crushed fragments.

Pere Laborde took him by the arm. "Come away at once. You must not stay here." He pulled the now unresisting Giovanni out into the hall and down to his room. The white garments hanging in the half-open closet, the rosary, the baroque wooden Madonna which stood in the corner, cast their spell on this Catholic soul in trouble.

"Oh Father," Giovanni said, "I got to tell you—"

13

AND CHARLES MIGHT have had a premonition of drama that very same morning had he heeded the signs. First, his secretary had broken out with a rash and the Duke's waking eyes saw, as their first impression, a series of oily lumps on the young man's forehead as he hovered over his master's bed.

"No, I won't speak to anyone," said Charles.

"But sir, it's the Princess Noldini. She's calling for the fourth time."

"That American bitch? *Sacre Dieu!* I told you I won't speak. Let her cry; it will relieve her bladder. Say I'm ill—Say I'm dead."

The secretary retired, distressed as usual, his eyes bewildered beneath the lumpy brows.

'I can't keep him,' thought Charles. 'He is diseased, the pig!' He raised himself on one elbow and as he did so caught a glimpse of Giovanni running down the stairs. 'Now where is *he* going?' wondered Charles. The thought of his protege having an appointment to which he felt he must run oppressed the Duke. "Idiot!" cried Charles aloud, and the poor secretary in the next room took the exclamation to himself.

To distract himself, the Duke began to think of his new scheme with Nigel. He pictured Giovanni putting up the miniature stage in various cities of the world. They would go on tour, to France, to Spain—like troubadours of old. He heard the roar of applause in his ears and saw himself bowing gracefully to the public after the performance, foot pointed delicately, arms full of flowers. He would be free then for months at a time, free of this house and its dark sister, free of Sheila—or would she insist on coming, too?

Just at that moment Charles had seen the rat. It had been lying near the bed, quite stiff and with its body horribly contorted. It must have come in through the double door while he slept, since surely there were no vermin in No. 5. It must have run from its lair, poisoned already, its bowels aflame. It must have writhed and leapt and gone with a rat's courage, fighting and convulsed, into the mouth of death. Charles screamed like a woman and the secretary came running to the door.

"Le rat!" shrieked Charles.

In her room, Sheila heard the scream and put more powder on her face. She would have loved her husband to be really in terror or pain, and the slightly affected cry set her dreaming: what if one day he truly needed her, was truly in fear or in despair!

Charles, once the rat had been removed, began the ritual of dressing. No one ever saw him stark naked, but how he managed it would have been impossible to say. There was a continual stream passing through his room: maids with fresh linen, visitors who wanted something from him, and his now bepimpled secretary. He was soon thrown into that hysterical state in which he would pass the rest of the day. He had taken black coffee and a benzedrine tablet. From time to time his face was twisted as the purge of the night before griped his bowels.

The long-eyed Candy, coming back from No. 7 after her lesson with Nigel, kissed her father on the brow.

"Bonjour, Papa."

Charles thrust out his lips in a kissing gesture and touched nothing. "You have had a good instruction?"

"Yes, Papa." She lingered for a moment, watching him brush his hair. "Papa?"

"Out, cherie?"

"Papa, who is this Giovanni?"

The Duke turned with a start. How utterly unlike Candy! He noticed her sleek head, her hair ribbon, her eyes fixed on him so clearly. Would she one day know the truth? Did she perhaps already know it? With one part of him he almost longed to tell her everything, yet he heard his nasal voice saying: "Ah, *cherie,* your mother is so difficult—everyone wants something from me—I am so alone."

With this well-known refrain Candy must have been content, for she went quietly away. Charles, while the telephone rang, the secretary hovered, the visitors arrived, kept repeating to himself: 'Alone, yes, alone, alone.' Eventually, with his toilet completed, he went down the hall to see his wife.

Sheila was ready for him. She was dressed to go out, in layers of uneven black garments and a fur coat.

"Where are you going?" he asked.

"Shopping. I must get another evening dress, and many things besides. I was just coming in to the office to get some money."

So that was it! Charles knew exactly what these words really meant. He knew his wife was saying: 'I'm not blind. I know you want to start that horrid puppet theatre and are supporting that charlatan and have plans to travel and have a good time. But, although we have a big allowance, ha-ha, my money is in trust, so—' So she would do her best to spend cash. She would buy her evening dress and it would hang in the closet, never worn—useless coin with which he might have done something for his pleasure. He ground his teeth but was helpless. They were both too far gone for an explanation; they could only attack and counterattack. Sheila was busy, pretending to fasten her coat.

"But *cherie,"*—Charles' voice was high—"I wanted to speak to you. You see, my friend Nigel is making us some dolls puppets, and we are to have a theatre for which Dali is already designing something. We will play Shakespeare and Corneille and Racine, all the great plays, and I want you—with your perfect diction—to speak the women's parts.

I have discussed it with several managers and soon we will begin our repertoire and get contracts."

Sheila almost let herself be seduced. How unutterably sweet to be his partner in this theatrical game, how glorious to enter into his life and become one with it after all these waste years. No longer to wait agonizingly, in her room while he slept, or among his guests in his absence. Yes, to be able boldly to say: "Charles, rehearsal is at eleven. Wake up!" To have her place and her right to say it. For an instant her eyes twinkled and a faint flush came into her cheeks. Then she turned aside. No, it was all a lie and would end for her as had his other schemes: in loneliness and tears.

"I don't want to speak the parts. I could never learn all of them, and your Nigel is repulsive. I hate him."

Charles would have replied but the secretary knocked at the door: "Mr. Orloff is here with the bed, sir."

Stanislav Orloff was the link between a well-known antique shop and Charles. It was all a system of cuts. The shop sold, Sheila bought, and the percentage, a large one, was divided between Stanislav and Charles. There were many petty expenses in the Duke's life, some of which were unexplainable.

"Come and see the bed," he cried, forgetting their argument and dashing out. He had long been awaiting this particular antique. Ever since he had bought his title, his will had been bent to forget that he was not Spanish but South American, and he had called to his aid a whole series of imaginary heirlooms: jewels that had his crest and that he had come to believe were really handed down in the family; portraits of ancestors in cloaks with swords at their sides, arched in the proud stance of Spain. Now Stanislav had found him this bed, and soon Charles would come to believe that he had been born in it.

At the moment two men were carrying parts of it up the stairs and into a little room off the office. This was the showroom and it was decked out with all the religious and material necessities of a duke's bedchamber—all except a bed, that is, and now it had arrived. The two men began to set it up, while Orloff, blond, Russian, ageless, spoke to Charles. The real aristocrat and the impostor, face to face. Orloff had been very young at the time of the Revolution, and so blue was the blood that coursed his veins that to keep his titles seemed a vulgar superfluity. He was interested only in having as nice a life as possible with a minimum amount of work, and in this respect he was a fair exhibit of Charles' salon. Although he had married a distant relation of the Duke's, he never came to No. 5 with his wife, perhaps because he loved her.

"Ah, je me sens que je vais tellement bien dormir dans ce lit. Yes, sleep well for the first time in years!" cried Charles, who had no intention of ever passing the night in the bed. "It will be like coming home."

Stanislav Orloff gave his hard wolf smile and smoothed back his blond hair.

'How beautiful he is,' thought Charles, and said aloud but in a low voice: "My dear, can you give me something right away? *J'en ai besoin."*

Orloff nodded and turned his eye towards the door through which Sheila was coming. "Good morning!" He spoke in the loud, cheerful voice that people use for sickbeds. "It's starting to snow," he said, and in his soul there came such a longing for snow, thick, deep, winter-long snow, that his expression froze into one of astonishment—so, occasionally, must winter animals in the zoo pause, their fur yellow and sparse, a white, glorious vision in their brains.

Charles caught the expression and merely reflected that Orloff often looked stupid. By now the bed was up and, turning to Sheila, he said: "There, *cherie,* isn't it a marvel?"

"Yes, very nice."

The sickly petulance of her voice set him off. "Very nice! You should take a tonic to stir up your liver. Very nice! It's a miracle, a wonder!—You!" he shouted to the workmen, "Isn't it a wonder? I am sure *you* understand."

The two men shifted and grinned. "Looks kinda small to me," said one, eyeing first the bed, then Charles, then Sheila.

"Depends if you want to get one person or two in it," said the other.

Sheila disappeared as though the hallway had swallowed her up. The words of the workman sounding in her ears seemed to throw upon her marital life an unbearable light. It was as when, in a thunder storm at night, a lightning flash reveals a stunted tree, black, tormented, obscene in the electric glare.

As for Charles, who was still admiring his bed, the workmen had said nothing to upset him. He tipped them both generously and sat down on the edge of his purchase. It was one of those ironwork filigree affairs, at once fussy and austere. Orloff was standing at the window, watching the workers outside in the street. Having finished their digging, they were presumably preparing to put the paving together again. The snow fell on their caps, and their sweaters were dusted with white. The living breath of each spurted like steam from their mouths and nostrils. One could almost see the brief words they spoke, written in the air.

Hearing her girlish, indefinite step above, Charles raised his head. "Candy's room is right over this one," he said.

Orloff turned and rested his round blue eyes on Charles' face.

"Oh, Stanly," Charles went on, "I assure you it is terrible to have a daughter. I am beginning to be afraid. This morning she was wearing a ribbon. A red ribbon, and braces on her teeth! That taste for scarlet, believe me, Stanly, when a young girl begins to have that, it is an indication!"

As he spoke, Charles caught a vision of Candy with rouged cheeks. 'But no one would look at her now,' he reassured himself. 'Poor child, so plain and dressed with so little becomingness.' Much better that way. Once on the market, he was lost. Candy would go, and he would be left shieldless, alone with his vampire, his Medusa, who turned his bones to jelly and sucked his sour humours to fortify her tears.

Charles had to go down to lunch, then, but the thought of Candy would not leave him, and afterwards he came up again to sit on his new bed, which had been covered in the meantime with an encrusted drape. Sitting there alone, he became impregnated with an idea that both pleased and saddened him. It occurred to him that this might have been the bed in which his daughter had been conceived; that here he had had, not Sheila, but a dearly, a passionately beloved, and that Candy was the fruit of their union. He sat there and cast his mind painfully back.

Oh that endless honeymoon, his wife's and his! He remembered the hotel suite with its cupid ceiling and silk walls. He remembered the bed where, with a desperate repugnance, he faced each night his virginal and awkward bride. He had been upborne by one hope then: he must, he *would,* make a child. Each night he prayed, gritted his teeth, forcing himself to erection by the desperation of his will. The vital seed, however, was missing and he felt it.

One day, waking in the morning very early, he had gone out on the balcony and looked down at the deserted Place Vendome. He had leaned his arms on the railing wearily, ready for tears, and a nostalgic sadness had caught him by the throat. It had been a hot and sultry night, and now the first freshness of morning was like a flower. Then Charles had noticed a dark youth, little more than a boy, walking along with his coat flung over one shoulder. He seemed such a free, unfettered creature, walking there in the dawn alone. Charles could not resist coughing to attract his attention. He had looked up then—swarthy face, black eyes, Indian, arching his breast upwards in one piece with his throat and his pointed chin. He had flashed his teeth in a smile at the melancholy man leaning over the balcony, but he had not halted his soft quick step and Charles, with a longing he could not control, had stretched out both his arms towards the upturned face. The boy had laughed when he saw that gesture: those two arms held out to him. He had laughed and gone on, still laughing, happy and gay, with his Mongolian eyes wrinkled and his chest arched.

Charles had returned to the luxurious room with tears on his cheeks. That night, faced again with the problem of his marriage, a desperation had taken hold of him. He ignored everything: Sheila's glance, furtive already from lack of love; her flesh above the girlish nightgown; the thin legs bending to his will. He had strained not to touch the breasts or the soft belly and had turned out the bedside lamp. Then, in the darkness, the Indian boy came back to him, laughing softly, with the cords standing out in his throat and the hair falling over his eyes. Charles had given a moan of despair and joy, and into the body of his wife he had poured the living drink that was Candy de Tudelos.

14

NIGEL WAS IN THE SALON of No. 5, his legs primly crossed, balancing a cup of after-dinner coffee on his knee. To one side of him was a woman of the type who is always being called the 'Best-Dressed,' and to the other was an antique Russian countess. The best-dressed woman's name was Lulu, and although she might have had another, no one ever heard it. She was in her prime: emaciated above and secretly spreading below, and she had on the uglier of her two well-known evening dresses. Lulu was actually a little shy and had covered it up with arrogance for so long that the scab had thickened and would never come off. Sensing that Nigel was one of Charles' new favorites, she troubled to be charming.

"We are so excited by your plans for the theatre!" she was saying. "Charles tells us that you get extraordinary likeness and that we shall all be represented." Here she turned her profile in a way that showed the hollow moldings of her cheeks.

"If everyone were only as lovely as you," murmured Nigel, basking in this land of arid make-believe and quite at home in it.

The antique countess, at hearing his words, lifted up a throat and chin of such raddled, forlorn splendor that the conversation was ended. Suddenly, Nigel saw them both quite clearly as if they were made of wax; not only them, but all the others in the room—the Bebes, the Booboos, the Nanos, robbed, one and all, of real flesh and stature. Amongst them, he felt himself a giant, and a surge of power mounted to his brain. Yes, he would reduce them all. Beneath his hands they would soften. When he so desired, their knees would be bent. A turn of the wrist would have them bowing before him.

"Certainly," he said, as though continuing a talk, "certainly it will be very interesting. But I must excuse myself. I must go back to my studio and work. We artists, you know." He rose, put down his cup, bowed to the two silent women and left the salon. His happiness was complete because he knew they could see him going, not down the stairs to the outer door, but up, and so, through to the next house.

'Ah,' thought the Countess, 'so I have come to this. I, who have made geniuses tremble for one kiss of mine (for she had once been the mistress of a well-known composer), now must lift my head to disguise my wrinkles from such as he!' Touching the best-dressed woman's arm, she asked as though her very flesh were questioning: "Tell me, Lulu dear, where are *they?* Where have *they* gone?"

"Who, Myra sweet?"

"They, the men!"

"You mean Nigel? Why, he's gone up to work. He's staying here you know." Lulu thought the Countess crazy with age or drink, but this did not prevent her showing her familiarity with Charles' friends by calling them by their first names. She wriggled uncomfortably. Her girdle was too tight and gave her gas, especially after coffee.

Nigel glanced out the window as he passed the Duke's study and saw the red lanterns wink against the snow. How glorious to be in this big house, to look out of the clear panes. Nigel paused only an instant; he really did want to work and he was experiencing again, for the first time in years, that, thrill of the creator with power in his hands. He walked to his room, switched on the light, and gazed with horror at the shambles within. Every bit of modeling he had done so far was ruined. The very table was dented and scarred from the hammer. Here and there a smooth arm, a leg or fragment of a face remained unshattered, as though in added mockery. A sour stench burned Nigel's nostrils.

He thought at first he must be dreaming and with the tips of his fingers touched the befouled and broken remains of his work. His mouth grew thin, not with rage but with fear. Here, where he had thought himself safe, where against all probabilities a haven had opened up for him, here of all places, the hand of an enemy was at his throat!

A flow of curses, rendered sinister by Nigel's metallic ice, poured from his lips. It was as though one of his own puppets were swearing. The room was darkened by destruction, by fear, and by the unknown presence of his foe.

Yet, was it unknown? Nigel stopped his cursing and hurriedly looked over the table and floor. A detail from the morning pricked at his brain. Yes, he was right, the image of Mrs. Puchini was either completely smashed or it was gone, for he could find no trace of it. Just then he heard footsteps on the stairs beyond his open door, and the young Italian, pale with swollen eyes, confronted him, clutching the waxen figure of Mrs. Puchini in one hand.

Giovanni stared for an instant at Nigel and then said thickly, with an almost comic drama: "My ma's dead, Mr. Neju."

Nigel saw that he was drunk, swaying forward a little as if about to commit some violent act.

Then, gulping, Giovanni repeated: "Mr. Neju!" and started to laugh.

Nigel felt his face burn. "Get out, you roughneck!" Strangely enough, Giovanni obeyed his command and went on through the hall and up the next flight of stairs to his own room.

So Mrs. Puchini was Giovanni's mother and she was dead! She must have died right after seeing him and that was why she had not brought the money he had demanded. Was it possible she had actually died through him? She had been so fat that her heart might well have stopped. Nigel wondered what she had said to her son. Giovanni obviously knew or connected something, and Giovanni and Charles—Nigel felt all his security leave him. A few minutes ago it had been so easy. Now, like a tightrope walker who had suddenly lost his nerve, he looked down into a terrifying pit. The faces of the guests whom he had believed to be in his power, faces to remold as he wished, to ridicule or to flatter, rose before him in imagination. They gathered with bored smiles and cynical eyes to watch his headlong flight. They had seen so many such accidents in Charles' house! And where would he find the force now to pick up the threads of his trade, his shoddy, charlatan occupations? The thought of his excursions on Broadway and his talks with perspiring women had made him wonder how he had ever been able to live at such a game.

He sat down at his battered table and tried to plan a defense.

"May I come in?"

Nigel gave a start and saw Pere Laborde in the doorway. "Yes. Yes, do." He noticed with anguish that the priest was not surprised, was even smiling a little. 'It has begun,' thought Nigel.

"He is very impulsive," said Pere Laborde without preliminaries. "That is Latin blood for you." He made an eloquent movement to indicate the damage. Pere Laborde was happy. He had not yet figured the means of turning this thing to account, but never mind, such situations were to be made use of. He knew how if anyone did: meekly, slyly, and ending, perhaps, with a greater hold on Candy's education.

"He was drunk," said Nigel.

Pere Laborde shrugged and let a hint of reproach creep into his voice. "And emotional too, of course. These Italians worship their mothers." Nigel, who had remained seated, let his hands turn outwards on his knees in a helpless and pleading manner, but the priest was not yet ready for giving comfort. "I wonder what our good Charles will say to this," he mused. "He was so happy at the work you had done."

"I can do it over."

"Yes, yes of course, and I hope this will not make him lose interest. He is so quickly discouraged, *le cher ami*—and he is so fond of Giovanni—Yes, he is sure to be very upset."

Nigel looked around him desperately and, clutching at any straw, said: "And the boy is very fond of Charles as well. So he should be, of course. He probably thinks the whole family are saints. I noticed him with Candy only this morning." On Nigel's part this was merely spadework for his future showdown with the Duke, but he saw that the present result was better than he had hoped. Pere Laborde's eyes flew open and the smug smile gave way to a sickly grimace.

"What did you notice?" In his anxiety the priest stooped down and plucked at Nigel's sleeve.

'So that shoe fits,' thought the experienced Neju. Aloud, he hesitated: *"Mon Pere,* I don't like to say too much, and you are not a man of the world, after all. I should not be forgetting myself." He rose, turned his back on the white-robed figure and strode about the room as though wrestling with discretion.

"But you *can* tell me! That is just what I am for, and it is my duty—and yours, too—to see that warnings are given before it is too late." The Dominican spoke in such a pathetically inquisitive and distressed tone of voice that Nigel felt quite at home. Here, in his room it might have been a woman, harassed by loneliness and middle age, begging for life at his hands.

"As you probably know," said Nigel, sitting down again, "as you *certainly* know my past and profession, you will realize that I am a trained observer. I am not a Catholic, but I believe priests only hear confession hidden from their—victim. Not I. We talk face to face. The tears are visible, the clasped, tense hands. By such signs I observe whether I am hot or cold, near the mark, or vice-versa. I have grown very acute—"

"For the love of God," Pere Laborde broke in, "don't give me a lecture, give me the facts!"

"Facts? I have none, if that is what you want. Yet, as sure as I am sitting here, those two young people are violently, physically, in love!" As Nigel spoke, all his fear of Giovanni found expression, and into that word love, he rang the corrupt timbre of his voice so that it shook in the air.

"Mon Dieu!" Pere Laborde could not repress the cry. His pale, not too clean fingers fumbled at the wool of his dress.

"Why do you care so much?" Nigel asked. The priest tried to pull himself together but it was too late. Those light eyes, shallow and cold, saw through his attempt. Nigel went on quickly: "No, don't give me the churchly reason. Save that for Charles, if you like. Here we are, both of us, in a stew over Giovanni. I know why he bothers *me.* The evidence surrounds us. But you, why should you worry?"

Pere Laborde opened his mouth and then, as nothing came out of it, closed it again. Even if he would, he could furnish no reply. He, a half-man at best, a priest in robes and a creature no longer young, why had this canker grown in him and what could he expect from it other than pain? Pere

Laborde as a young seminarian had known a certain lust, had even, in its womanless form, known gratification. He had simpered and flirted in his white skirts. Even now, when he saw just what attracted him—But Candy! Her long eyes, the flat, blind, snakelike side of her head! Ah, it was too much! There was no reasoning! He met Nigel's questioning gaze.

"Nigel," he said, "Neju—whichever you are—there is nothing I can tell you, nothing except that the Bible is right about them. *We* lead lives that many people think vicious, but let me tell you that when you have drained the cup, when you have tilted it to the end—Oh that last bitter drop! The lees of vice, a woman!" He bent and thrust his face close to Nigel's. "Why, even in burning Sodom," he cried, "who knows what eyes looked out towards that salt column and were filled with tears."

Nigel laughed. He leaned back completely relaxed. "I don't believe you. This is just a sort of change of life you are going through. Take yourself in hand, Father." He paused as if for reflection. "Just think," he continued, "how powerful we are!" On the word powerful, Nigel dwelt with a sort of soft intensity. He added: "Why, we rule the world. Politics, art, religion—"

But Pere Laborde spread his hands hopelessly and turned to go. Then he stopped and said: "Leave it to me. Charles will act. I know him. He does not yet realize what he is going to suffer at the hands of his child." He seemed to think of something else and his manner changed. "Yes, leave it to me, but before I speak to him, there is a matter I would like to look into. In any case, we are both agreed that such a hotheaded young man must be placed out of the house and away from temptation. *Bon soir, mon fils!*"

Nigel had nothing further to say. He knew that the affair would now be in far more passionate hands than his, and some pendulum in his nature swung back in sympathy towards the stupid youth with his raw charm and clumsy opportunism. Such as he, were victims. Giovanni was like his mother; make an image, fill it full of pins, and he would suffer. Nigel reflected that he need not have been so frightened after all. He looked about at the disordered room and began to pick up the fragments of his work and put them in a pile. With a towel he wiped up the traces of Giovanni's nausea. When all was in order, he undressed, hanging his suit carefully. He brushed his teeth and nails in the adjoining bathroom, put wrinkle cream on his face and got into bed naked. Then he read his horoscope for the next day and found that he was to have a sentimental disagreement and clinch.

He was still not sleepy, for the excitement of the last days, plus tonight's incident, had acted on his nerves. So much going on around him! So many people feeling strongly about one thing or another! He wished that a feeling, any feeling other than that of self-preservation, would penetrate the coldness of his temperament. He wondered if the barren years had not set a seal upon him which could not be broken. Perhaps, for each woman whom his words had made tremble, there was a toll taken from the life-heat of his own emotions.

Nigel got out of bed again. He went to the mirror and examined his body in its nudity, as though to force from it the secrets of his spirit. Was it the harsh light that made it appear so dry? He lifted his arm and looked at the underside of it. Here the skin was free from hair, fine in texture and so thin that the veins crossed it like blue netting. He rubbed his cheek against it and the stubble of his beard left a red mark. Thc parody of this secret act, the miming of a lover and his beloved, left Neju oppressed and lonely. He put on a dressing gown and went out into the hall, hoping to find Charles in his room. The Duke, however, was out or downstairs, and

Nigel went on into the top regions of No. 7, which he had never before visited.

A dim light hung from the ceiling above. Once a chandelier, now there was but a naked bulb hanging over the stairwell, swaying slightly from a dozen draughts. The bulb, harsh and dim at once, lighting the narrow black depths between stair rail and hall, down, down, made Nigel reflect that this house was not very different in appearance from the one he had lately quitted. Here, too, they were all boarders, only they paid in a less easy coin, a fluid cash whose weight was never put on the scales, to whose face no sign was affixed. The priest, Giovanni, himself, Nigel—for each this same basic money, although each paid it out differently. Nigel shivered. He could hear the wind blowing in under the doors and could feel it sharp as a knife on his ankles.

Giovanni must sleep in the front room, he thought, and entered boldly. The boy had fallen into bed with his clothes still on and was sleeping heavily. The light from the hall lit up his face and, as he was one of those people who never quite close their lids in slumber, there was a white gleam between his lashes. He was lying on his back with one leg bent and no covers over him. Even from above, Nigel could feel the heat from those powerful inner thighs and upraised arms. He did not remember why he had come. Was it to force some answer out of this brute body, or simply to look down at another victim who was to be destroyed by his charlatan magic? Nigel sighed. He would have liked to lie down beside Giovanni and sleep, but he did not dare, so he went back downstairs to his own neat bed.

15

ON THE FOLLOWING MORNING, Pere Laborde listened intently from his post in front of his room. His head with its morbid nostrils and tonsured scalp was raised. He clasped his hands nervously together. Yes, there it was: the step of Candy, the step of a long-legged bird, a little maimed. How absurdly it wrung his heart! He waited until she had knocked at Nigel's door and heard the charlatan's voice saying:

"Come in!"

Then the priest left off his watching and mounted the stairs. He wondered anxiously if Charles were awake. It would certainly have irritated the Duke to have seen his white parasite so early, but luck was with them both, the Duke was still asleep and Pere Laborde went safely through to No. 5. Even the secretary, busy at the telephone, did not see him, and it could be guessed by the back of the secretary's head and from the movements of his free hand that someone was saying he absolutely must speak to Charles.

As Pere Laborde escaped into the hall, he glanced into the ancestral room with the new bed and noticed a rosary hung over one edge of the ironwork. His religion had turned to hypocrisy long ago, yet whenever he was thus reminded of his faith, a perfume seemed to waft against his soul and penetrate it. How sweet that call had been! How beautiful the Christ whose feet he had so often kissed! Pere Laborde could recall every tear of contrition, every act of penitence and joy. Yes, a veritable spring of joy had welled up every morning in his heart. What had become of those feelings? Had God withdrawn from him, or was it he who had withdrawn from God? Of course, he was still a priest. There was a monastery awaiting him in France. He came over periodically to lecture and preach in America, and always before had managed to return. Now, as the weeks wore on, he doubted whether he would have the strength to do so again. The other day he had received a letter demanding explanations for his delay and had hardly been able to read it. He would have to answer it nonetheless, sooner or later.

Arrived at the top floor of the house, Pere Laborde cautiously opened the door to Candy's room. If anyone—the maid or Charles' wife—saw him, he would say he was fetching a necessary book while his pupil wrote out an exercise. The room, however, was empty. It was neat and warm despite the snow that glittered on the window sill. No clothes were lying around and the bed was made. Yet it was indisputably the dwelling place of a young girl. The air was scented with her fragrance, her uncertainty, her immense expectancy of life.

And there, lying on the bureau, was the leather diary he had given her with its strong lock and gilded pages. He took it quickly, hid it in his sleeves and made for the door again. There he almost bumped into Josie, who was entering with a pile of mended garments. The servant's eyes, distorted and red-rimmed behind their glasses, narrowed in suspicion so that her lashes bent against the lenses. They looked to Pere Laborde like two ugly insects seen through a windowpane, their thin legs crawling along the glass. "Good morning, Father!"

He could not, or would not, return her greeting and went on down to find Charles now awake and talking on the telephone. The secretary saw Pere Laborde this time and gave him a harassed smile. The secretary's forehead was by now absolutely covered with blotches and some had even come down onto his cheeks. It did not occur to him that one of the reasons for Charles' irritation could here be accounted for. He was so naive, so earnest, that he could not conceive of its making a difference to another man. Yet, when Candy passed by on her way to lessons, he went into agonies of self-disgust and shame.

Pere Laborde did not trouble to return the secretary's smile. He hurried on to the ping-pong room where he taught his pupil and prepared for her coming. Then he got out his razor—he always shaved with a straight blade—and cut the broad strap attached to the lock on the diary. It was a shame to spoil the leather, but there it was. He remembered giving it to her and with what care he had selected it to be just like her: new, rosy and fresh, filled with smooth blank pages. With what joy would he have marked every one of those pages had he dared! In the end, he had inscribed it simply: To my beloved child, Candy, from her father in Christ, Pere Laborde.

Now a stab of sorrow pierced him, for he saw that she had covered the inscription by pasting a drawing over the first page. It was a reproduction from some art magazine and on looking closer he recognized it as one of Goya's etchings. It portrayed a priest sitting in a chair reading, and underneath, in Goya's handwriting: *Puede ser que sea bueno.* Candy had added to this an exclamation mark—a childish defacement which seemed to Pere Laborde the height of insolence. Also, the figure resembled him, and he had no doubt that Candy had noticed it. But why the exclamation mark? The words themselves—*It is possible that this could be a good man*—were ambiguous enough, written, one would think, in Goya's very bile. But Candy's additional! Did she really wonder if he, Pere Laborde, were a good man, or was it merely sarcasm? More clearly, was it possible that she felt any doubts about his being bad? Every day they played a game together wherein he was sanctimonious, she meek, and both false. This game was the real aim of his existence, so much so that when, by a quiet remark, she won a round, he would have given a year of life to get even. Pere Laborde rarely admitted these things to himself, and most often he actually thought of Candy in just the way he pretended to behave towards her—that is, with unction and affection.

Hearing a step on the stairs, he put the diary down hurriedly. It was she! He held his breath for the moment she would discover his theft. He was thirsty for her reaction. To drink the nectar of her fear, of her shame—this would be the most sublime taste he had ever had on his tongue.

Candy saw her diary at once and saw, too, the broken flap. So it had happened! Somehow she had known it would and that her betrayal would come by this priest's hand in the end. All the blood in her body seemed to shift, to turn in a convulsive movement, as when a vessel half filled with liquid is set abruptly another way. She did not speak but sat down, still looking at the pink booklet with its light brown wound. She could not force her eyes away from it even though she expected Pere Laborde to make immediate reference to its contents.

"My child," he said, "we have finished *Hamlet* and I wonder what we should start next. Moliere? Perhaps a Balzac novel? What do you think?"

Candy was thrown off by this irrelevant speech, and then she thought: 'He is not going to say anything.'

"I have no preference, *mon Pere.* Just as you wish."

He tried to detect even one sign of pleading, but her tones were as cool as ever. He looked at her closely. Her eyes, set so smoothly in her face, showed no strain and her forehead was serene. Only the mouth looked pinched and dry, yet that might well be the cold. "Perhaps we should do *Paradise Lost,*" he said. "We shall have to do it one day or another. Have you ever thought, my child, that for all of us there is a sort of paradise which we lose?"

"You mean, on earth?"

"Yes, yes, on earth. We have it and we throw it away and do not realize, until after, that it was paradise. You, for instance, living with your dear Mother, your witty and stimulating Father, having your room, your books, your girlish dreams—Ah, my child, that sounds like paradise to those who have had thorns to trend on."

"And shall I, do you think, have thorns to tread on?" asked Candy. She saw his head snap up so that his nostrils offered themselves naked to her gaze.

"Yes," he said, "thorns to tread on. Thorns under your feet, under your bare feet!"

"Shall you put them there, *mon Pere?"*

"God will put them there."

"But you, *mon Pere,* are the instrument of God, are you not?"

Pere Laborde got up and put his hand on the diary so that his soiled white sleeve fell over the leather. "Let us put off our lesson, Candy, until this afternoon. I have work to do."

Candy stood in her turn and gathered her books together. "What time shall I come, *mon Pere?"*

"I do not know. I shall send you word. You see, I shall probably have to have a talk with your father, so I am unable to fix an hour. He has so many appointments, *ce cher homme.* I must wait his convenience." Here he made an habitual movement, a sort of smile with his whole body. He had waited so often in vestibules!

"I understand." The young girl nodded as she spoke in her usual quiet voice, and left him there, with his hand still covering her diary.

As she mounted the stairs, Candy felt sick. She started to blush in a way that is known only to the adolescent. The words she had written stood out in front of her eyes and, when she put up her hand as if to stroke away the vision, she felt her forehead wet, icy with sweat, although her veins seemed to burn the flesh they served. And now her whole being yearned towards the top floor where Giovanni lived and must at this moment be. If only he would pass close to her now! She longed to feel him near. Candy knew that all her life as it had been until now would end with Pere Laborde's disclosure of her diary. He was right about losing one's paradise.

Then she thought, teeth clenched: 'No, it wasn't paradise after all. It was a dull hell with only one flame—which will now be put out! Besides, I wanted this to happen, didn't I, when I wrote the first page?"

Yes, she had half wanted her diary to be read, although she could no longer recall why. Only then, she had never loved.

'Love,' thought Candy to herself, and the word tasted hot in her dry mouth. What was he doing up there? Dressing? Reading? She knew he came down to the salon every night among her father's guests, so he would be tired in the mornings. She pictured Giovanni sleeping with his chin dark, his black hair marking his face, while outside his former comrades worked in the snow. Why had he not stayed among them? What had drawn him into this dark house, out of the bright, free, crystal world?

She repeated to herself the word love, but the original warmth was gone from her tongue and the sickness came back.

Charles was not there as she passed through the double door. His bed looked rumpled and grey despite the fine linen sheets. Neither was he in the study and Candy was disappointed. For some reason she had wanted to see her father, to say good morning to him in a daughter's peaceful way, to receive his kiss on cheek or brow. The secretary was sitting at his desk writing and, as she passed, he jumped nervously to his feet and then immediately sat down again. The problem of whether to rise or stay seated for the daughter of the house was insoluble, so he tried to do both, and now, as usual, found a big blot of ink on the page. Charles disapproved of typing. It was plebeian. He had chosen this particular young man for his Gothic hand. It made things much slower, especially if one spilled ink on a page. Candy, who usually smiled at his dilemma, and even went slowly on purpose, did not notice it now.

"Do you, by chance, know where my Father is?"

The fact that she said 'by chance' and 'my Father' instead of Papa was enough to make him stammer: "Y-Y-yes, in the b-bedroom."

"I've just come from there." Candy spoke patiently.

The secretary meant, of course, the stage bedroom, but did not know how to designate it without impertinence. If he said 'other' bedroom, it would seem to mean Sheila's. In desperation, as he saw her standing there waiting for his reply, her eyes fixed, so he thought, on his bumpy forehead, he broke out: "The f-fake one."

"Thank you." Today Candy was aware of nothing and she went out and knocked at the closed door beside the office.

"Come in." Charles was sitting on the wrought-iron bed, the tips of his pointed shoes barely touching the ground. He was wearing no jacket and his collar was open at the neck.

Against the white shirt his face looked grey. One eyelid jerked. Candy was just the person he wanted to see. "*Cherie,* come and look at my bed! You did not see it yesterday." He caught her hand and kissed her fondly as she stooped.

"It's beautiful, Papa. It just suits you."

"I knew *you* would understand." And then, in a rush of sympathy and affection, he cried: "I do it all for you, you know, all this." He waved his hand towards the ornaments, the paintings and furniture. "Not for myself. I want you to be proud of your family and of your noble blood." This speech was not true, but he felt it to be so at the moment, and it came as near to a confession as he had ever made her.

Candy was silent a while and then she said: "Papa, do you think being noble or not really makes a big difference?"

He was about to answer emphatically, but then he thought again of that Paris dawn and of that dark, free-striding creature who had, in a sense, engendered Candy. "If the father is a gentleman," he said, as though he meant *seigneur,* "if the father is a gentleman, then, even if he takes a peasant girl as wife, it makes no difference. That is, if she is beautiful and graceful."

"And was Mama beautiful and graceful?" Candy could not have told, even in her innermost depths, whether or not her question was sincere.

Charles stared at her a moment, his mouth a little open. She could see the tips of his eyeteeth, two pointed tusks which pushed against his upper lip on either side. He truly could not think what Sheila had to do with the conversation. Then he recollected himself: *"Cherie,* what idiot things you ask! I have known your mother only one year and nine months longer than you."

When Candy got to her room she carefully removed her shoes and stretched out on the bed with her arm up over her face. She found herself exhausted and fell at once into a profound slumber which lasted over an hour. Then, while still in that trancelike state between sleeping and waking, she saw herself once more in the dream garden about which she had written in her diary. This time she entered and, kneeling directly beside the fountain, pressed her forehead to the stone brows of the cyclops. She felt his warm, single eye pressing between hers, and from his mouth, like words of longing and pain, the water spouted onto her thin dress and wet her throat. She knew it was important to decipher the meaning of those watery words, but they were so liquid, so endless, with their soft, unfathomable speech poured out upon her own mouth!

"Tell me!" she cried. "Tell me!"

Then, turning her head, she looked at the house in her dream with its reflecting windows. Yes, there was the broken one on the second floor, and there, too, was the face. Yet something was changed, because the window was crossed by black perpendicular lines, as of iron bars. They obscured the face behind them, casting dark, brutal shadows across the features.

Candy got up and moved towards the gate. "I must go now," she sang out in a sweet, false voice, "and besides, how can I tell if it really is you, with all those bars over the window?"

Candy at this moment distinctly heard herself close the garden gate with a click, but because she was in that middle, semiconscious state, she knew with some other part of her brain that what she heard was the key turning in her door.

Someone had locked her in from the outside.

16

** Last entry in Candy's diary [made on the morning of Pere Laborde's visit to her room]:*

.... Snow! Last year I would have spent hours at the window, writing poetry (which I write very badly) about the weather in connection with my soul. Today I should hesitate to connect myself with anything so ethereal. Have I a soul? If so, she has flown away, leaving a burning hollow in the space she once occupied. I can feel it all the way up the center of my chest. No, it's not hollow; it's filled with him. With him! Shall I write his name? Giovanni. There—now no one can read this until after I am dead, or anyway old. Giovanni, Giovanni! Yes, and when we were in the room of that white-haired creature, he pressed against my shoulder and I felt it afterwards—literally, I mean, my shoulder blades were sensitive all day. I can explain it better. You know when you are undressed and rub your cheek against your shoulder? It is the cheek that feels, isn't it? I mean, whatever kind of skin you have on your shoulder, it's the cheek that feels it. Your shoulder can't tell at all whether your cheek is smooth or coarse. Well, yesterday I was sure it would be the other way around, but of course it was on my back so there was no way of trying it out.

Soon I must go down to my modeling lesson. Perhaps Giovanni will be there. It sounds funny to want to go on seeing a person when the *aim* is something one didn't enjoy at all! Or, if I really didn't, why this desire to feel him *over* me, over me with his hands pressing down? Not like he was; something different, I don't know what..................

Charles, as he read, was still sitting on his ancestral bed, his toes tapping the floor. When he had finished, he lit a match and touched the candle which stood on the night table. Taking the socket in his hand, he set the book aflame. The golden edges withered and turned black. A great orange flower burst into bloom where the Goya had been pasted. Charles dropped it on the carpet and the priest would have liked to step on it and put it out but, as he approached, Charles shrieked:

"Laisse-le, imbecile!"

Pere Laborde jumped nervously away. In any case, it did not burn. There was the smell of the scorched rug and then the flame flickered out. The leaves were too thick, between paper and linen.

The Duke shuddered. He felt icy cold. So this was what happened when you had a daughter! The combination of it sank slowly into his mind: Giovanni, Candy—a terrible picture of them together came to him and would not go away. He saw the texture of their skins and their mouths swollen with desire. He imagined their broken cries, breathed in like breath, one from another. And Candy's legs, which he had never entirely seen, now appeared to him wound around the tough, straight hips of her ravisher. He gave a cry of anger, all the more bitter in that this vision which tormented him actually excited him at the same time so that his limbs quivered.

Then he thought: 'Giovanni! I brought him into the house from the gutter—' "Yes," he cried aloud, "and I'll send him back to it. He'll see what it is to meddle with what does not belong to him. I shall punish him!"

The priest gave a sickly smile. "He seemed like such a nice, sincere young man."

"Nice! You call that nice? When he has ruined my child? She might as well be dead! Sincere, eh? If I were strong I would force her to drink poison!"

"I just said 'seemed.' *Voyons, Charles,* she has committed a great sin, but the Church teaches that there is confession, penance and pardon—"

"Church!" cut in Charles. "What do I care about the Church! I am not praying now. I am going to act!" He looked at Pere Laborde and said: "How ugly you are. How stupid. I shall send you to the country with Candy for a year. No, I'll send you back to your monastery. That's where you belong. She shall have a duenna. She shan't be seen again until she's eighteen. I am still master here." He worked himself up: *"Imbecile!* Wretch! Go and get Nigel!"

Pere Laborde hurried off and Tudelos leapt up from the bed. Now at last fury held him, top to toe. No more pain. They should all feel his heel on their necks. To everyone of them he could bring misery and shame and he would do so! A black lump of gall filled his chest. He was stifled and his face grew congested. He thought for a moment that he would die and tried to call out. His cry, mixed with the thick gall in his breast, would not carry. His pointed shoes shuffled on the carpet and he fell back on the bed. All this was, however, half acting. One day he would have a stroke in earnest and he knew instinctively how it would feel. With a kind of masochism he sometimes brought on this rehearsal of what would eventually be his death.

Nigel came in, a set smile on his lips.

"So," gasped the Duke, sitting upright instantly, "I gave you my trust and you betrayed me! For the sake of our youth I took you in and wanted to give you everything. Now see, you have not protected the one creature whose purity was vital to me!"

Charles was starting to enjoy himself at this point, but it was too emotional. Nigel found something in the hot blast which rendered him secure. He grew calm and lost his nervousness of a moment before.

"How dare you!" he said coldly, coming up to Charles and staring into his eyes. His own, so expressionless and grey, made the Duke's dilated pupils shift. "Who brought that Italian here?" Nigel continued, "And for what purpose?" Then, as Charles made no answer, he went on: "You seem to have more or less the same tastes, your daughter and you. A strange kind of incest!" Seeing that his darts had struck fully home, he put his hand on the other's shoulder. "Come, Charles, I am your friend. Your life is your own, never fear, and you are quite right about being angry. So what are you going to do about it, aside from shifting the blame?" Then, slowing his words and shaking Charles' shoulder gently, he said: "By the way, do you love him?"

Nigel's voice, thin and metallic as a castrate's, gave Charles pause. "Love him!" he echoed, and jealousy like some ferocious beast gnawed at his heart. Giovanni, young, brown, with that rebellious lock over his forehead. Giovanni with his abysmal, his divine ignorance. Giovanni the docile, who had bent to his will. Charles could remember those white teeth bared in pleasure of pain, and the girlish fringe of lashes. Yet, in that somber other house, even there, Giovanni had managed to find his own ecstasies and had wrested from its setting the hidden jewel, the chief stone in Charles' collection, the only one that was real, through and through; his inviolate diamond. How had they met and when? Perhaps he, Charles, would never know.

He forgot Nigel and went out of the room and into his real bedroom to stand at the door of No. 7. A fresh and nubile breath wafted down the hall through the motes of dust. He flared it, lifting his sharp profile against the gloom. 'I must see Leonine,' he thought and went at once to the telephone.

Leonine had been at outs with Charles for several days and had not seen him since her greeting of his protege. When they had phoned each other last, she had told him of her social infidelity and he had slammed down the receiver. Now she answered his call from her bed, in which she was lying with pads over her eyes, attired in pink silk.

"Charles! Why haven't you called me? Are you still angry?"

"Cherie, I am coming right over. I arrive!"

She yawned and listened to the receiver click. In ten minutes he came in the door and sat down beside her on the bed. It was a strange thing that he, to whom women, the womanly parts of them, brought disgust, was never repulsed by Leonine. On the contrary, he was more relaxed and at ease with her than with anyone. He looked her over impartially: crumpled nightgown and sheets, one arm up over her head, and the mouse-colored hairs of the armpit clinging to her skin on either side. Although she troubled with eyepads, she had not completely removed the eyeshadow of the night before, and there were traces of lipstick on pillow and chin.

"I must get up," she announced, and without bothering about her guest threw off the covers and put her feet to the floor. She sat for an instant at his side. "You don't look very well, my poor Charles," she said and, rising, opened the closet door.

He replied pettishly: "I am ill. Yes, ill. Imagine it, I have taken a real traitor into my house. It is awful!—Leonine, he has made love to Candy."

"Candy!" She was really startled and came out from behind the door with her stocking half fixed. She was one of those women whose legs are slim and straight enough to wear garters without wrinkles at the knee, and she had one stocking already stretched smooth to where she wanted it, high on the thigh. The other was wadded around her ankle. Aside from this, she was naked. Charles did not care, nor even look.

"Yes, he seduced her!"

"Or she seduced him. She is a determined creature." The woman went back to her dressing, thoughtfully.

"No, no Leonine! I wanted her to be perfect. You know how I felt. She, at least, should be something that came out right in my life. God knows, you too, what my life has been—and is. I wanted her to be pure."

"You make me angry," said Leonine, cutting off this flight.

"You're all the same. You worship purity like a bunch of old whores. 'Oh lamb of God that taketh away the sins of the world.'" Half clothed by now, she twisted a scarf of red and dark blue satin around her throat and sat down to do her hair. "Why should she be deprived of her sweet little sins just to whitewash yours?"

"A young girl should know nothing, should be innocent as the dawn, otherwise she is a monster!"

"You mean, a rival," she said, looking at him in the mirror. "How stupidly you talk. A young girl is a step between child and woman. She is meant to be loved, to be taken, and that way only can she grow up. Besides, a young girl means virgin and is automatically pure. When she is no longer the one, she is no longer the other." Having finished patting her hair in place, Leonine dabbed on a little cream, a little powder and a great spray of perfume. Getting up, she put on the jacket to her suit and became immediately superbly and expensively dressed. The satin gleamed against her chin, and the careless swing of the skirt emphasized the length of her thighs. She walked in her high heels with that brutal elegance of hers. And under it all was the unwashed skin, the lips still gory from yesterday's feast. As she approached him, the two perfumes, natural and artificial, were still at war on her body. She spat at him like a cat:

"Now tell me the truth!"

Charles started and clasped his hands as though to pray. He stammered: "I am so jealous! I suffer!"

"Poor Charles!" She put one of her hands on his head, almost tenderly. The touch brought up his rage.

"Don't you see?" he said, "I can't bear it. I can't! I won't! He was *mine!"*

"But my dear, how can *I* help, aside from sympathy?"

"I want him to be punished," he cried. "Ruined! There is nothing, no lengths to which I am not prepared to go." He leapt up with his hands still clasped and walked up and down.

Leonine was unimpressed. "Charles dear, stop that and let us talk of other things. Have you read the paper yet? I haven't. Let's take a look." She reached for it where it lay on the bed. "Ah, so they signed. I thought they would. And look, *Broken Shadow* got good reviews. I suppose Eddy will be impossible from now on. Pay attention, Charles, I want to tell you about Eddy last night after the opening." She recounted her anecdote with such a mixture of cruelty and good humor that he was swayed back under her domination.

She flicked the pages of the newspaper idly and said with only half a mind: "These girls! Every day they seem to arrest more, soliciting—but you know, Charles, I saw Jim Sloan the other day; you remember he used to work for the *Daily News,* and he says it's a racket." Here Leonine put her hand on the Duke's shoulder and forced him to stand still and face her. "They frame them," she said with peculiar emphasis.

"Really? Who does?"

Leonine waved a vague hand. "Oh the plainclothes men, I suppose." She turned the force of her eyes, opaque with age, on his and continued: "But anyone could, of course. It would be easy."

Charles seemed tired of the subject after that, and restless again, although in another way. He took her hand and kissed it. "I must be going. There are twelve people for lunch and Sheila is useless. Will you come? No? Well, try and drop in tonight. Bring Rogers if you like. You are wonderful; an *emerdeuse,* but wonderful."

17

AFTER THE EMOTION of his drunkenness, his violence, and his tears, Giovanni slept like a child. He did not open his eyes until the following afternoon and missed lunch. On waking up he felt gloriously relaxed, with not even the shadow of a hangover. The light from the sun on the fresh snow outside washed his room. Every drain in the street, every window sill and roof edge was dripping, cascading snow water. The sound was like a promise, repeated again and again, that winter was passing and the next season would be spring.

A few minutes after he opened his eyes, Giovanni started to recall the events of the previous day. Had it been he, tramping about the city with tears on his face? Had it really been necessary to fly into such a rage? In the light of a new day his behavior seemed to him absurd, and he was glad at least that he had refrained from running to Charles, like a baby.

"Sure," he reasoned, "she knew the guy. Perhaps he read her fortune. So what?" As for the wax figure, wasn't Nigel always making likenesses of people he had met? Why, just yesterday, they had laughed over that old countess who was around the other house with her screwed-up face. Nigel had caught the expression just right, and the figure too, flaunting a skinny nothing! Besides, Giovanni had seen his mother as she lay dying and no one had come in and killed her while *he* was there. All the rest was silly, superstitious old-world nonsense.

Nigel was sure to be angry with him for the damage he had done on the preceding evening, but at the same time, Giovanni could not believe in anyone's anger this morning. He himself was too blameless, too young. He jumped out of bed and threw off the clothes in which he had lain all night in his drunkenness. They stank of liquor, strong and vomited, and he wrinkled his nose in disgust as he ran into the shower. It was Charles who had taught him the pleasure of bathing, and Giovanni was proud now of his clean body. He watched the water driving against his chest, sculpting the black curly hairs on his skin. Only the puffiness of his eyes betrayed his debauch. The water soothed them and brought down the swelling.

Around three o'clock, dressed and shaved, Giovanni hurried downstairs, intending to get something to eat. Nigel, coat in hand, stood at the first stairhead.

"You're going out?" asked Giovanni, hanging his head slightly out of embarrassment.

"As you scc."

"Do you want me to pose for you later?" Giovanni flashed the older man a winning and coquettish smile. He continued: "Nigel, I'm sorry I broke your things. Honest, I didn't know what I was doing. I was drunk."

"It's of no importance," said Nigel without expression, passing carefully so that they should not touch. Nigel wanted no part now of this doomed creature. Just as a healthy person avoids his diseased friend, so he avoided Giovanni, whom he knew to be condemned and ruined.

Giovanni heard the coldness in Nigel's voice but he had made his apology and felt better. As he passed through the double door, his spirits rose again. Anything might happen in this grand, beautiful house. He might even catch a glimpse of—Why, what was that great thump of his heart? 'Candy,' he said to himself, and again he felt his heart thump up against his side.

Charles was not in his room and the front hall too was empty. "Hello!" he greeted Harris the butler, who was just finishing with the luncheon dishes in the pantry. Harris turned his head slightly but made no reply. Giovanni, undaunted, kept up his air of joviality. "Anything to eat around here? I'm hungry."

Still without a word, the butler opened the door of the refrigerator and brought out a plate of cold meats. From a bowl he ladled out some Russian salad and then planked the plate down in front of Giovanni as one might do before a dog.

"Gee, it looks good." Giovanni could not bear that anyone should dislike him. His voice wheedled for Harris' approval. His teeth flashed, then he started to eat uneasily.

Harris finished drying and putting away the last dishes and turned his fishlike stare onto the youth. "You are not to dine in the dining room tonight," he remarked flatly.

"Why? Who said—"

"Boss's orders." Harris cut him short. It was only to social inferiors—equals did not exist, only superiors and inferiors—that he ever used the word boss, and a day ago he would never have employed it when talking to Giovanni. He knew his place better than that! A favorite, while in grace, is a superior.

Giovanni, although not very perceptive in these matters, felt that something was amiss. He was like a horse who scents a wolf without ever having had cause to fear one, or even having seen one in his life. No direct knowledge causes him to bolt, yet he pauses, nonetheless, and opens his eyes and lifts his head.

"Where am I supposed to eat then?" asked Giovanni.

The butler shrugged. "Suit yourself." Reaching into his pocket, he drew out a five dollar bill. "Here," he said contemptuously, "the boss said to buy yourself a meal with this." He threw it down on the shelf beside the sink and then leaned back against it, staring at Giovanni. He made an ugly figure in his shirtsleeves, with his cuffs rolled back and a striped apron tied around his bony hips. A thin smile drew down his nose. 'Well, sonny,' he thought, 'I guess it was good while it lasted.'

Giovanni could barely eat under this enigmatic gaze and Harris' smile disturbed him as did his motionless stance. "Know where Charles is? Has he gone out?" Giovanni called the Duke by his Christian name in pure bravado and felt foolish on doing so.

"We don't use first names out here," said the butler. "If you mean the boss, I know nothing of his whereabouts and he gave me no instructions to tell you anything other than what I have just told you."

This correct and stern speech was pointed up by the common word, boss, which took on the sound of a deliberate insult. One could see Harris hardly ever used it and that it was the equivalent of the words some men permit themselves among prostitutes.

Giovanni was by now openly startled by the butler's manner and, as Harris stayed where he was, leaning against the sink with his arms crossed and with that pale, triumphant stare, Giovanni broke out into absurd boasting. "I guess we're going abroad soon," he began, leaving an unused space for the other to reply. "Yes sir, we're going to travel all over. Nigel is going to finish his dolls and we're going to set up a theatre in all the cities. The Duke says we'll have plenty of publicity in every language, with all our names on posters. We'll be the real actors, see? We'll speak the words behind a curtain—Shakespeare and all."

At this, Harris made a small sound. Giovanni flushed, blinked his long lashes and cried: "Sure! You don't believe it? Ask your boss!"

The butler crossed one foot over the other. "Is Miss Candy going along, too?"

The naming of Candy seemed to run up Giovanni's body like a chill. It was as though somewhere in the depths of his being a stone had been thrown into a deep pool. Even said thus, spitefully from thin lips, the syllables added one more ripple to the disturbed waters. Ah, that flung stone cast around it such a glamour, such a glitter towards the shores of his soul!

Nonetheless, with his primitive self, his animal scent, Giovanni knew Harris for an enemy. "Why?" he asked boldly and in too loud a voice. "What's *she* got to do with it?"

"What indeed?" murmured the butler.

"She's only a schoolgirl anyway," continued Giovanni. He knew the subject was dangerous, yet could not leave it alone and had to exploit it past all prudence.

"Is she only a schoolgirl?" asked the butler in mock surprise. "Now I should call Miss Candy very grown up for her age, but then, I'm not a real connoisseur of women. I suppose you are. I suppose you've measured her up, jack-deuce, from top to bottom."

"So," cried Giovanni, "you want to insult me! That's what you want." Coming up close, with clenched fists, he shouted: "Top to bottom! Yes, I've measured her, and I tell you she's a schoolgirl and you leave her be, do you hear?" His swollen, choleric neck and the great fork of vein cleaving his forehead turned Giovanni into a satyr, a pathetic satyr whose forest is cut down or far away and lost for good.

Harris made no move and kept to his place, with his arms crossed on his chest, his right foot over his left. Giovanni, hearing no reply and seeing no change, felt his wrath die down until he was left standing there with his face foolishly thrust out and his fists clenched. He turned on his heel and made for the swinging door.

"Don't forget your money," said the butler, and had the pleasure of seeing Giovanni turn and shamefacedly take up the five dollar bill before leaving the pantry.

"I guess you've earned it all right, you fool," said Harris to the door as it swung back and forth.

Giovanni found No. 5 still empty. The salon reeked with smoke and perfume and had the deserted appearance that rooms take on after a crowd of people have left at once. Charles, no doubt, had taken them all with him to his box at the opera. It was Saturday, which meant there would be a matinee, and Giovanni could picture them filling the box to overflowing, the men sharing the chairs. Why had he, Giovanni, not been asked in this case? Everyone knew he loved the opera. In fact, one of the greatest advantages of his new life was that he could succumb publicly to this taste, which had before been considered out of the ordinary and queer. But perhaps they hadn't gone to the opera after all. There were plenty of other things. Giovanni knew that having neglected his guests for hours, Charles was capable of carrying them out of the house in five minutes in a storm of enthusiasm. Wherever they arrived, there would be too few chairs and too little space, yet no one would care. They were with a rich man and, given luck and a little elbow grease, they might and their faces in the next day's papers. So both sexes kept their eyes bright and their lips slightly parted for a smile.

Giovanni mounted the stairs and, as he passed her door, thought he heard Sheila stirring in her room, like a rat in a closet. He knew by now that he definitely did not like Charles' wife. She was unlike any other wife or mother he had met. She was weird, with her floury face and pink-rimmed eyes. He looked on her with contempt, and in his native frankness recognized her in her coarsest terms.

Once in his room, Giovanni did not know what to do with himself. The sun had gone but the day was not over and it was not nearly time for dinner. Wandering around the top floor, he found an old gramophone and a pile of dusty records. He played them one by one until darkness set in. Old words of love, old, weary phrases of sophistication and surrender. Giovanni felt a physical distaste of all that the songs implied, of their lubricity which deprived conquest of its rough thrill. As for him, it was night by now, and fresh air would do him good. He put on his overcoat, almost new though secondhand from Charles, and went outside.

Darkness had stopped the melting of the snow, yet it had not entirely frozen. There was a mere puckering of the water in gutter and puddle and the air was damp. The construction looked wet and uncomfortable despite its red lanterns. He would be glad when it was finished, because it restricted him to see his former mates working and to have to pass them if he went out. He shrugged his shoulders and looked up at No. S. Charles' good house was alight. While Giovanni had been playing records new guests—and probably the old, as well—had turned up for late tea and for dinner. The curtains were not yet drawn, because Charles liked people to be able to look in at the splendor of his domain. Giovanni could see the guests milling around and made out Charles in their midst. Then he cast his eyes up to where, like a clear star, Candy's window shone onto the street.

She was there! He saw her profile and her lifted arm. She was dancing. All by herself in her room, gravely, in an academic manner that was the opposite of abandon, she went through the few steps of Spanish dancing she had been allowed to learn. She raised her arms, rounding them and snapping her fingers. She arched her back and beat out with her heels an exact rhythm. Giovanni could not see the minor points, but he could see her advance and recede, and the motions of her arms.

Beautiful, solitary Candy, alone in her room, suspended like a star in the night. And between them, the watcher and the watched, there was blood, there was violation and the glutenous mixture of life. Giovanni put his hand with its fresh-healed scars up to his face. It would be a long time before those marks had disappeared. Perhaps they never would. He felt again the force and anger which had driven him into her body. The taste of her ravishment was once again on his tongue, bitter and salty and mingled with the floor's dust.

Candy had stopped dancing and stood cooling her forehead on the glass of her windowpane. How pale and removed she looked thus, as though seen through water. How had he ever imagined that she could be his wife? What did he want with her from now on? Giovanni could not even reflect, he only felt his chain. Now, something in the way she stood brought back his feeling of unquiet. She was so captive looking, not subjected exactly, but completely caged. One could feel behind her the door closed and locked. Giovanni hunched his back.

She turned and moved away from the window and he saw Josie come up and pull the blinds.

18

IT WAS CLOSE to seven-thirty when Mr. Puchini got home from his rounds. He dreaded this moment; the empty fiat with its dirty dishes piled in the sink, its smell of solitude and spilt wine. He mounted the stairs wearily.

"Mr. Puchini?"

The voice made him jump. He looked up to see a man on the landing. The man's dark suit and wing-white hair were too sleek for these carpetless stairs with their unvarnished railings.

"I want to speak to you if I may."

Mr. Puchini did not much like the voice with its odd ring, and the words were overpolite. Yet he could think of no excuse, and some company was better than none in this the loneliest hour of his day.

"Come on in," he said.

It was dark in the flat, so he touched the switch and examined his visitor. Nigel was well dressed. That jarring note in his face, the repulsive coldness, was accentuated by his clothes. It is said that a woman with a defect must so exaggerate it that it becomes her greatest weapon. Nigel, after his stroke of luck, had used this technique and had succeeded in looking dangerous in a suave way. Now he smiled.

"Don't be uneasy, Mr. Puchini. I have only nice things to tell you."

Mr. Puchini, who had not actually been so before, now coughed, touched his mustache to see if it were still there, and awaited a catastrophe.

"It's about Giovanni."

Mr. Puchini jumped. "Where is he?" he cried. "Is leave right after my wife died and never come back. Giovanni's a good boy. Why he leave me? He's say nothing."

Nigel, while the man spoke, looked around. So here was where she had lived, that fat woman, and here was her brutal and stupid husband, whose words ran together and who probably longed to take off his shoes.

"Giovanni's all right, Mr. Puchini. He's doing well. I think he wanted to make good before coming home. You see, there's been a fine job offered him, a job with big pay and he's anxious to take it. He says if he gets it he's going to ask you to live with him"—Nigel chose his next phrase deliberately—"off the fat of the land. He told me that after his mother died suddenly like that, he felt he just had to make good."

"Make good? Make good! But he was doing fine. We had everything we need."

Nigel realized that it would not be as easy as he had planned and the man's next words confirmed it:

"It's something bad, that's it! That's why he went like that without *adio!"*

"My dear sir, don't excite yourself. Giovanni, I am sure, would never do anything underhand. It's just because of his honesty and good character that he is wanted for this particular position."

Mr. Puchini hesitated. His visitor certainly did not look like a thug, despite his unpleasant qualities. Perhaps Giovanni really was on to something honest as well as lucrative, and would come up in the world. "I don't understand," he said. "Why you come-a-to-me?"

"Well, Mr. Puchini, it's this way," said Nigel, with an attempt at ease. "This job's confidential. He's wanted as chauffeur to a very important person. Now this person is wealthy and goes abroad once a year. He has to be careful whom he hires, and although he thinks your son would be just right for the price, well, there are a few minor difficulties."

"Why? My son has very good character. Everybody around here he's-a-tell you the same thing!" Mr. Puchini was now on the defensive. "He's done nothing to be ashamed of, not since he's-a-born!" Mentioning the birth of Giovanni struck the father sharply in his memory. He recalled his wife in her black dress getting off the boat, the profile of her body swollen and distorted. How lost they had been at first! Pregnancy had seemed like a rock, a dear, familiar landmark. Yet his sister-in-law had been kind to them, no denying it.

What if she did make her money out of men? She had been a good girl for all of that. Ah well, she was dead now, murdered by her pimp, they said, and his wife was dead too, and all his children were scattered or dead, as well. He sighed.

Nigel leaned forward. "Mr. Puchini, how old is Giovanni?"

Mr. Puchini wrinkled his forehead and Nigel recognized the grimace. "Round about eighteen," he said.

"Ah, you see! That's just the trouble. To take his responsibilities, to travel and all that, he should be over twenty-one. That's why he sent me to you. He thought I'd be able to explain better than he and he wants the job so much. His future employer, you realize, would not dream of taking on anyone underage."

Mr. Puchini's black eyes were dense with these reasonings. He turned up his palms questioningly.

Nigel said: "You have other sons, Mr. Puchini, don't you?"

"Sure, three.' Angelo, he's-a-go back to Roma. He no like the U.S. ever, and his girl she's-a-wait in Roma. Then I have Giancarlo in Silenas, California. He's-a-working in garage there. Also I got Philippo. Only he's-a-dead."

Nigel started. This was unhoped-for luck. "How old would Philippo be now if he had lived?"

"About twenty-two, twenty-three. Was born in Italia."

"But that's perfect!" cried Nigel. "Do you have any papers of his? Birth certificate, passport?"

"Sure I got," said Mr. Puchini. "He was too young to get a passport but I got the birth certificate and naturalization papers too. They give them back to me after he fell."

Nigel permitted himself a smile. "Don't you see," he said, "how lucky that is? Just you give those papers to me. Philippo can't need them anymore and Giovanni does. A little work and we'll make your son out the right age and you'll be living off the fat of the land."

Mr. Puchini tried to concentrate. What would it be like to live off the fat of the land? Would it make him less lonely from five-thirty to eight? Was there something wrong in the stranger's request? He could not explain to himself why he felt unsure. Yet it would never do to let slide the future of his son. He made a last demur. "But why, why he no come himself?"

Nigel brought a conscious patience into his voice. "Giovanni is a boy, Mr. Puchini. He wanted to come home well off, with a smart uniform and money in his pockets. He was crying when he heard he was too young and I told him I'd see to it all myself and that he was not to worry."

"But who are you?" asked Mr. Puchini.

"I," said Nigel drawing himself up, "am the butler."

Mr. Puchini's fight was over. This man's occupation settled everything. It accounted for his stiff face, his careful clothes and speech. Of course he would become strange—everyone did in that situation, as could be seen in the movies. Mr. Puchini relaxed. "Sit down," he said. "Have some wine while I get the papers." He pulled out a chair for his guest and poured a big glass full of wine from a jug on the table.

Nigel lifted it to his lips. It was terribly sour, as if the inside of the grape skins, acid and harsh, were rasping his tongue. Mr. Puchini slouched off. Nigel heard him moving in another room and then the rustle of papers. He leaned back in his chair and took another sip, puckering his mouth. After the rich life he had been leading, this crude wine was salutary. It pleased him to be drinking it here in the home he had wrecked once and would now destroy again. It moved sharply down his throat. It was good.

By the time Mr. Puchini returned with two grimy papers almost severed by creases, Nigel had finished his glass. His host poured another and then one for himself. Nigel, watching him throw the heavy jug over his wrist and elbow, was again reminded of Giovanni. In the father, thickset and strong, a trace of the son's litheness remained. The unity of his movements, the useful beauty of his acts, traced a pattern in them both.

"Let us drink to your son," said Nigel and they raised their glasses together. Then he could resist no longer: "I am sorry to hear of your recent loss," he said.

Mr. Puchini blinked and his mustaches drooped. "She was fine woman, Mister."

Nigel leaned his elbows on the table. "What was the matter? She died suddenly, I hear."

"Yes, is right. She's-a-go to bed one night and never get up no more. She sweat her life away, that's what! Doctor said her heart he's-a-sick for a long time. He's-a-tell me my wife caught a cold in her chest and this weak heart he's-a-collapse." He drank again, a long gulp. "I never noticed no cold," he said.

Nigel was staring at him, fascinated. He felt the quality of his share in the woman's death, acid and delicious as the wine he was drinking. Yes, while he had been dragging out that solitary and sordid existence, a woman had died because he had said to her: "Thou shalt die!" No, not quite that; he had given her a choice, after all. It was she who had preferred to die. Because, surely she had the money. People did, when it came to choosing like that. He recalled Candy's diary, which the Duke in an agony of rage had let them read. It mentioned a sum given Candy by Giovanni. Nigel threw back his head and laughed.

"Why you laugh?" cried Mr. Puchini, jarred to the marrow of his bones. This visitor's unexpected grimace, the un-manliness of his neck exposed by laughter, and the callousness of his timing, shocked and enraged the widower.

"Oh I *am* so sorry," apologized Nigel. "You see, I'm not used to wine and I was just thinking what fools doctors are. Do forgive me! I know how deeply you must feel your loss."

Mr. Puchini was thrown into embarrassment by this apology. "She was a fine woman," he muttered defensively, putting his hands apart to measure the breath of her departed fineness. Then he sniffed, slung the jug over his arm and refilled both their glasses.

"Did Mrs. Puchini appear to keep her health right up to the end?" asked Nigel. With every probing question he became more feverish. He could not control a slight twitch in his cheek, a trembling, really, inside his mouth, which was puckered from the wine. His head felt light.

"Sure she was healthy! She was never sick even when she got children. When Giovanni came we have no time to get to the hospital and she's-a-make us a big pasta afterwards right away!" He pushed back from his lips the stained and dripping ends of his mustache and pondered. "Still, she acted funny, in the end, never spoke or anything. I think she's mad because I lose a little money playing cards. I think 'Who cares, a woman changes with the wind, wind blows, anger flies away'—but then she go to bed. She's-a-never get up in this world." He shook his head at the mystery. "Jesu-Maria!" he exclaimed. "How that woman she's-a-sweat."

"Sweat?" asked Nigel softly, savouring this detail. At the same time he ran his tongue voluptuously over his teeth which were rough and blunt from the wine.

"Sure!" Mr. Puchini, too, relished this. "Why Mister, you shoulda seen it. The sheet he's-a-wringing wet and all her hair, her black, long hair—" He caressed an imaginary mass. "Why, it's like she's-a-swim in the river all night."

The gesture of caressing drove Nigel to a pitch of exasperation. It expressed everything he detested: the numerous children, the frequent, over-robust copulation, the preposterous admiration of Mr. Puchini for his grotesque mate. He asked cruelly: "Did you get a chance to say goodbye to her properly, Mr. Puchini?"

Mr. Puchini's eyes grew dark. "No," he answered. "She's-a-never say goodbye." Something he had been trying to forget came back into his mind. "Is believe I'm someone else," he said sullenly. "Sometimes I think she—no, she was an old woman. But it's funny, she kept saying the name of another fellow. Yes, and she talked about radiators. I guess she just got crazy." He paused a moment and then the relish came back to his voice. "She's-a-scream," he said.

"She screamed?" Nigel was now trembling in every limb. So she had screamed! She had called on him as on God and screamed and dissolved in her own fat. All of her had dissolved: her hideous breasts, her horrible, rolling buttocks, her sagging belly folded down on her thighs with the results of love. "Oh," he cried shrilly, pushing out his trembling fingers on the table, "how I *wish* I had been there!"

Mr. Puchini's face was scarlet with wine and these sadistic words that should have infuriated him, excited him instead. His eyes, already those of an old man, glistened and his mouth was wet. He jumped to his feet and brought his fist down on the board. "Yes, by Jesus!" he shouted, showing his broken teeth. "She's-a-sweat! She's-a-scream! She's-a-scream! She's-a-sweat! Like-a-love! Like-a-when we kiss! Like-a-when-a-the kids come out." He started laughing and Nigel, still sitting, laughed with him.

"I'm not too old," cried Mr. Puchini, beside himself, laughing and choking. "Giovanni gets the job, I get another woman. Fat. Fat! I'm a man. I'll take her to bed. I'll make her sweat. I'll make her scream—Ha!"

Nigel's nerves felt like a frail tree held by wires at the joints. At each juncture the wires now rubbed together and with every word the Italian uttered the whole tree shook. Suddenly the charlatan stood straight up with his arms by his sides, opened his mouth and gave a shriek of hysteria.

"That's right! That how it was!" choked Mr. Puchini, watching him admiringly.

The tree inside Nigel quivered and the wires rasped.

Mr. Puchini, incited to imitation, now shrieked too, in falsetto parody of his wife. Then he stopped abruptly and sat down with a heavy look on his face and his cheeks running with the dregs of his mirth.

Nigel, too, became silent and returned to himself with a terrible effort. Like an automaton he took up the papers and put them in his pocket. Then, without a word, he opened the door and went out, leaving Mr. Puchini sitting at his table.

The cold air dried the moisture on Nigel's face and cleared his brain. How had he ever feared the son of such parents? He knew now that Giovanni could have done him no harm with Charles, yet the revenge he had helped plan was all the more sweet; revenge of the injurer rather than the injured.

The next day Mr. Puchini received a telegram: "Come at once Giancarlo very ill," and the wire also provided for the fare.

Charles must have had a friend in Silenas.

19

ON THE DAY GIOVANNI left No. 7 forever, he found a note pinned on the double door leading into No. S. He saw it when he came down in the morning. It said: "I am ill. Please do not disturb until tomorrow." From the handwriting one could tell that the secretary had written it. Giovanni was disappointed, as he would have liked to see Charles and felt a subconscious need of reassurance. Yesterday there had been the butler's insolent command that he not appear at dinner, and now this. He read the note again. Was it curtly put? Oh well, he shrugged, tomorrow would be time enough.

The double door's being closed gave the whole hall a different look, bare and poor. Giovanni wondered how he was to eat and what to do with himself, and also, where were the other guests of No. 7? Were they in exile too? Nigel he dared not disturb after the latter's chilly reception of his apology. Towards the priest he felt a certain bashfulness because of his tears, his passion, and his sobbing confession of hatred, which had grown absurd in twenty-four hours time. He went back to his room whistling loudly just to show that he existed. His feet creaked on the stairs and the atmosphere was gloomy and deserted. In these corridors how many lonely steps had been taken by boys such as he? Steps leading away from all that was familiar. Giovanni could almost hear them, could almost see the procession of young men mounting to the same room. For a moment he pictured himself as a ghost returning to a familiar scene. It was as though he had already quitted it and been replaced, not once but many times. Would another really sleep, bye and bye, in the bed where he had lain? Sleep and receive the visits of Charles? Of Candy? Candy, coming with her awkward gait, her hands clenched. Some power had drawn her into his arms; some fluid, burning inside her heart. Could she look at another boy in that room ever and fall beneath him to the floor?

"There's only one can get there first," thought Giovanni, to comfort himself, and was startled because he had said it aloud. He shook himself angrily, but the depressed, moody feeling remained. After all, it was his second day of solitude.

On reaching his room, he found an envelope half under his door. It contained another five dollar bill, a new one, folded sharply. The envelope, too, was spotless, and this added to his feeling of isolation. It was as though no human hand would bring him comfort. Looking out the window at the deserted Sunday street, he almost wished that the workers were in the construction. It would be better than no company at all.

Just then a street singer passed, forcing the season. His cheeks, even from Giovanni's post, were thin with the starving winter, and he was followed by a woman carrying a child and a tambourine. The singer, who was obviously of the Latin race, was singing a Neapolitan street song. He was a tenor and his voice was true. Behind him, now and then, the woman beat the empty tambourine across the crooked elbow which encircled her child. She completely disregarded all rhythm of the song. So they passed slowly by. The man's starved cheeks gave him a predatory air, proud and aloof. Even his eyes appeared to be set sideways, like a hawk's, so that he would never need to turn his head. From further on up the street a coin was thrown and the singer, coming up to where it lay, passed without acknowledgment. But the woman stooped with her burden. She picked it up, bit it between her front teeth, and put it in her pocket. Neither of them looked up. Soon they had turned the corner and were out of sight, although the song lingered on for a while, melodic and full of nostalgia.

This scene, for some strange reason which he could not define, filled Giovanni with sadness and with regret.

Later, he put on his coat and went out. He ate at a drugstore and went to two movies in succession afterwards. The luxurious sets of the second movie cheered him a little because most of the people around him had never been in a really rich man's house, and he had. He lived in one, almost. At No. 7 it was not quite like living there, especially today. Today it was like living nowhere at all. Also, in the movies, people who were rich led entirely different lives, and the women, it seemed to Giovanni, were unlike any who came to the Duke's: they were sexy and the men thought them sexy and fell in love with them. Actually, Giovanni was seeing on the screen a woman he had met in Charles' salon, but he did not recognize her.

Breathing in the darkness like cows in a stable, the Sunday crowd drank in the Hollywood cocktail, Giovanni among them. It was the season of colds. The crowd coughed and hacked, releasing into the overheated air a mingled odor of menthol and mucous.

Giovanni did not get home until after dinner and then he found somebody waiting for him in his room. His visitor was a boy of around sixteen or seventeen. He had mouse-colored hair and his blue eyes were wary and coy. He spoke with a very stiff mouth, perhaps to correct some weakness or quivering of the lips, and his chin, although it did not recede, was unusually small. He had spots.

"You're Giovanni," he said in a low, hurried voice. "I got a message for you. Your father wants you."

Giovanni was startled. "Who the hell are you?" he asked.

"I work evenings in the store downstairs from your father."

"You mean the delicatessen? What became of Jim then?"

The boy kept his eyes turned downwards and replied in the same low, colorless tones: "I'm new. Your father sent me. He couldn't come himself. He said he'd explain when he saw you."

"Oh yeah? And how did Pa know where I live?" Giovanni asked suspiciously.

At this question the boy looked up and fixed his gaze somewhere to the right of Giovanni. He said as though reciting a lesson: "Your father told me where you worked. I came to this street out front yesterday." He made a sort of ducking nod towards the window and continued: "They told me you were in this house. I came here today. I been waiting."

"Well, I'll come with you," said Giovanni and, added truculently: "But I won't stay. I'm sleeping here tonight, so don't get thinking different."

"It's nothing to me," said the boy. "I'm just doing your old man a favor." He took his short wool jacket from the bed and put it on. Giovanni had not yet removed his coat and both boys went downstairs without further words.

In the lower hall the priest stood as usual, a white, silent spy. "Going out for a walk with your friend?" he asked, trying to give no meaning to the words.

"My father wants me. He's not my friend."

The boy gave a tight-lipped, secretive smile at this, as though embarrassed yet pleased at being spoken about. "Sure, his father wants him," he said in hurried tones which implied that the smile had been an indiscretion for which he must atone.

"Ah," said Pere Laborde and, moving forward a step, opened his mouth to say something else. Then he changed his mind and merely clasped his hands convulsively between his wide sleeves as if they were cold.

Giovanni, before he left the house, caught a final glimpse of those nostrils which seemed to eat up the priest's face. He wondered why he had not noticed before that the Dominican disliked him.

The atmosphere was better outside. It was one of those blazing, moonless nights, cold and clear. One could almost drink this air into which the stars' light threw stinging bubbles. The boys walked swiftly eastwards and did not talk. Soon the sidewalks grew rougher and the houses less well kept. In some cellar, fixed up with glass and plush, a band was playing. From the street, only the saxophone came out clearly; now and then a metallic theme lifted meaninglessly into the night, a brass mouth thrust towards the stars. Plaintive, naked, passionate, the notes gave Giovanni the feeling of a prayer left unanswered. The pauses in between were waiting for a reply that never came. The stars looked down because they were set that way. Their faces were oblivious. The saxophone thrilled Giovanni's nerves yet aggravated the feeling of isolation he had had all day.

Abruptly the shadow of the elevated straddled Third Avenue, distorting the sky. The street lights were dimmer, with black patches in between. In one of these, the younger boy paused as though to tie his shoe.

"Wait for me!" he called out in a plaintive voice and Giovanni halted impatiently. He could see the boy's curved back in its stiff coat and then, without knowing how it happened, he found two arms around his neck and a face against his. At first he just stood there, feeling the arms pressing on either side of him and seeing in the darkness two white eyeballs, as though the irises were rolled up. It was an incredible moment, like a dream, and in its midst he heard a cry, coming perhaps from himself. He could not be sure.

Then a blinding light flashed on and a rough voice said: "O.K. Come along with me!"

Instinctively, Giovanni started to run, but his arm was held fast and he was jerked around.

"Get away, would you, you son of a bitch!" He half fell from the impact of a blow above the eye. Whistles sounded.

Giovanni did not pass the night alone and the other inmates of his cell served to reveal to him his own state. That he was now considered one of such threw him into despair; he had passed their like since infancy with a callous and deliberately hard-boiled laugh. He had been put with three drug addicts, a Negro and two whites. The Negro was very tall and completely enslaved by his drug. His mouth was slack and hung monstrously on his chin and he was slimy with sweat. The whites were sweating too, and one of them must have been past his time for a shot, since he could not stay still an instant. He was bald and the whole top of his head was covered with sores, as were the backs of his hands, which jerked continuously.

Giovanni lay down on an empty cot and turned his face to the wall. His eye throbbed. Once he asked himself why he had been arrested but the answer was so unbearable, so dark in its implications, that he simply could not cope with it. As the night wore on, he thought that despite their ravings and their strange, repulsive odor he would willingly have changed places with any of his cell mates, even the suffering one whose sobs and wild groans would have kept anyone awake. How simple was their case. They had taken this or that; an injection, a tablet—but him, what about him? What forbidden poison had been injected into his blood? What tablet had he swallowed without knowing? Or did he know? Was it possible that something so without pleasure, so mercenary and matter-of-fact, could be a crime? Giovanni had until now given surprisingly little thought to the axis on which his new life turned. It had seemed to him an accident, to be put up with, that was all. Yet it was not trivial. It had been no accident.

'Or do I really know?' his mind repeated in a panic, and then retired like a frightened rodent into the darkness. It was no use thinking anything yet.

At this point in his torment another man was put into the cell and Giovanni turned to look. The newcomer, after glancing around him comprehensively, crossed over to Giovanni's cot and sat down on the edge of it. He walked with the soft, supple, yet heavy tread, the debonair tread, of someone who had known many prisons all over the world. One side of his mouth was twisted higher than the other and this, although it had actually come about through torture, gave him an engaging grimace. He had been arrested on this particular night for drunkenness or, more precisely, for insulting a policeman, and he did not act drunk now. Yet his opening words were strange.

"Do you know," he began, "that the moon has just come up?" As Giovanni only stared at him sullenly, he continued: "Yes, come up, and do you know that if a person has worms—as I have often had—they strain towards a full moon? It makes them uneasy. They squirm and fight inside you." He passed his fingers through his soft limp hair which was thin on top. "Oh how drunk I am! I wanted to make a point. One should always do that in prison."

"I don't see what the hell worms have to do with it," muttered Giovanni, turning away again.

"Ah yes, worms. That's right. Well, what I was going to ask you was this. What about the worms in corpses? When we are dead will we stir in the full moon? Will our putrescent flesh tremble?" His voice, low and sweet, had in it the merest hint of accent, but one could not know its origin. Now he appeared to have done talking, for he got up and fell on an empty cot nearby.

Giovanni waited for a few minutes and then rose and stood over the newcomer. "Say, Mister," he demanded, "they can't put you in without telling you a reason, can they?"

The man squinted up at him. "My name's not Mister," he said. "Not Mister at all, although it might be Brother."

"Yeah? O.K. But I didn't do nothing."

The man turned his head restlessly to and fro on the cot. "It depends," he said. "Are brothers equally guilty?"

"Oh can't you talk sense?" cried Giovanni in despair.

At this the other put up his hand and touched the boy's cheek in one of those tender gestures which can be made only by the ultimate, the complete man. Then his hand fell away. He was asleep. Giovanni stood over him for quite a while, and for a while, too, felt soothed.

Giovanni was taken downtown to the Tombs in the early morning, and he was so cold and numb that he did not regain his wits until he appeared in the line-up. In this motley company he looked quite at home by now with his unshaven chin and damaged eye. The eye was completely closed and his long lashes were stuck to the swelling beneath by a yellowish paste. In the sleeve of his overcoat a tear showed the lining. His hair, dirty and greasy, fell down on his face. He hung his head.

"Next," called someone.

"Giovanni Puchini," said a voice.

"Picked up for what?"

"Sodomy. Caught corrupting a minor."

Giovanni tried to get his brain to work. "Say! I'm a minor myself," he cried.

"Do you answer to the name of Giovanni Puchini?"

"Yes."

"According to your own papers which you were carrying at the time you are twenty-two years of age."

Giovanni was about to shout wildly that it was not true, that it was impossible. He looked desperately from the policemen to the people sitting out front. He never shouted anything, however, because, there, sitting quietly in the sordid hall among the rest, was Candy de Tudelos.

For an instant their eyes met in some sharp meaning. Then Giovanni said in a low voice from which he could not keep the quiver of despair and fear: "Oh have it your way. Have it any way you goddamn want!"

Candy got up and left the room, holding in her pleated skirt with one hand.

20

NOW SHEILA HAD done it after all, had gone against both what others expected of her and what she expected of herself. She had gone through the double door into No. 7. What call, what impulse moved her heart, she could not say. Perhaps it was only that she had hovered too long between the known and the unknown, and now the hours allotted her for ignorance were run out.

She had waited a moment more in the double doorway, hesitating. Her pale face sent out into the gloom no luminous ray. The skin was too tired, too corroded by tears. Those monstrous tears of Sheila's! Such tears are the blood of the nerves. No wonder they spoil the cheeks down which they run. Sheila's hands clasped her upper arms on both sides in an attitude which crushed her bosom and rendered her shapeless. Her reddish hair was badly combed and her thin, girlish legs were slightly apart. She was listening. Lately she had felt that this dark house into which she gazed was encroaching upon and coming into her own dwelling. It was no longer content to be let alone. Its dim halls were eating up the fair, polished corridors of No. 5. Its boxlike rooms were filling the chambers like huge coffins. She did not want to understand its secrets, but they would not let her be. They were beginning to murmur in her ears.

It was during the last two days that this situation had become actually acute, ever since, in fact, Candy had been locked in her room. Charles had explained the reason for this to his wife and she had agreed that it was impossible for the girl to carry on flirtations at her age. Yet, through their conversation, as always, the undercurrents dragged. She felt their violent, dangerous pull beneath the surface of her brain. Sheila had not yet been to see Candy.

Now it was after midnight. All the guests had gone, and Sheila had stood listening on the edge of No. 7. Had she heard a voice above? Or was it pure instinct that made her step forward and up those unknown stairs that ran parallel to her own? Once in, she had no sense of strangeness, and small everyday thoughts crossed her mind. 'I must see to it that these stairs are better cleaned,' said she to herself, and: 'How that light up there swings! It must be dangerous and it's not half bright enough.'

She went slowly but without the slightest hesitation up the stairs and along the top hall to what had been until that evening Giovanni's room. The door was closed, yet light streamed through the cracks into the dim corridor and Sheila heard noises. She recognized her husband's tones, although he had never spoken such words to her—if they were words, if they were not groans, if they were not the cries of beasts—Sheila at first stood very still in front of the door and then softly turned away. In midstairs her foot slipped, by accident or by design, so that she fell with a crash against the banister. Two things happened: first Pere Laborde, who had been somewhere in the lower regions of the house, hurried up, and then the door above opened and Charles came out in a foulard-silk dressing gown.

"Qui est la?" he cried. "Who is there?"

"It is I." The little bird of a voice flew up to where he stood leaning over the stairwell. Half on her knees from the fall, Sheila could see Charles above her, his hands clutching the rail, his dark eyes fixed. Then he appeared to execute a dance. His arms gestured. His body swayed to emphasize his words.

"Ah, *cherie,* is anything wrong? Stanly Orloff is here. He came by just as I was about to go to bed. He wanted to discuss an auction with me. He was so tired, poor fellow, I told him he could take a shower in the room upstairs."

All those waving of hands, those twistings of the torso for this prosaic speech! Sheila made no reply, but in a curiously elegant movement rose to her feet. Pere Laborde was standing on the step below her. Deliberately she lifted her hand and gave him a heavy blow across the face. She hit him with the inside part of her fist, which she had clenched convulsively, and the marks of her knuckles sprang out on his skin. His eyes watered. His mouth puckered beneath his nostrils and Sheila threw back her head and gave a high, nerve-wracking laugh. Then she passed him and went back into No. 5.

Candy, in her room, was not yet asleep either. She had been lying there breathing in the crisp, star-shot air with her head pillowed on her elbow. She felt herself to be in a period of suspension which deprived her of rest. No one, aside from Josie, had been to see her since her imprisonment, and Candy had not wanted to speak to the maid. She had preferred to amuse herself: to dance, to read her books, to stare down at the construction in the street below. She too had seen the street singer and had been touched by an undefinable emotion towards that lonely hawk man who drew behind him his little world through starvation and winter. A kind of envy crept into her heart. He was not afraid, this male animal, although he had nothing. He did not fear to love, to beget, to support—She would not have thrown him money for all the world.

As to her own predicament—she was waiting, that was all. Candy felt so whole, so locked in her being, that she did not see what anyone could do to her. 'It may be,' she thought, 'that I shall be sent to the country for a few months with Pere Laborde.' But no, Pere Laborde made up a part of her father's court and so would have to stay. Perhaps a governess would be found for her, some stern, sad creature who would be no match for Candy.

At the same time she wondered what had been said to Giovanni. One could hardly lock a full-grown man in his room. Anyway it did not do to brood about it, one must wait and see. Candy rested, but her body felt tight and smooth. She was like an athlete of whom some effort will soon be asked. His sinews gather. His heart pumps deliberately to strengthen all his veins.

Then the door opened and Sheila stood there, key in hand.

"Why, Mama!" said Candy, surprised.

"Here is the key." Sheila's voice was as fretful as ever and her tones refused to make of this an unusual occasion.

"Are you letting me out, Mama? What am I to do with my freedom at two o'clock in the morning?"

Sheila made no reply to this question but simply placed the key on the inside of the lock. Then she said: "You know he's gone. I think they've done something to him." With that she left quietly and prosaically as she had come.

Candy felt as though a shaft had struck the center of her body. She quivered in her bed. "Done something to him," she cried. She leapt up and ran to open the door.

Sheila was halfway down the stairs. "Done something to Giovanni, you mean?" Candy's voice was sharp and high. "Done what, Mama?"

Sheila turned her white face upwards for an instant. She shrugged her shoulders. "*I* don't know."

Candy went back into her room and lit all the lights. She pushed the bell beside the switch for Josie. There were bells to the servants' quarters in all the rooms, but this was the first time Candy had ever used hers. She pushed it again, pinching her lips together to curb her mounting panic.

"Miss Candy!" Josie was like a ghost in an old faded dressing gown with two thin braids along her jaws, and turned-over slippers.

"Josie, tell me what they've done to him!"

The bewildered woman came in and closed the door behind her. "Who opened your door, Miss Candy? Your father?"

"Josie, never mind, it's all right. Mother did it. You must tell me what I want to know. Tell me, Josie, *where* is Giovanni?" She had both her hands on the woman's shoulders and her nails were digging into their meager flesh. The servant's eyes were squinted against the blaze of light and had turned into watery slits. Josie could barely see without her glasses.

"Calm yourself, Miss Candy. None of this is your concern."

"No, you shan't get out of it like that, my dear!" cried Candy. "This time you must take sides! Take *my* side! You know and you are going to tell me."

"But, Miss Candy, I tell you I don't—"

"You *know!*" The young girl turned her eyes directly on those naked slits so that the pupils of one reflected the other's. "Listen, Josie, I will never forgive you if you don't tell me at once. Do you hear? Never! You love me, don't you? Well, then, tell me!"

Josie put her hand up to her face. "Oh, Miss Candy, yes, I'll tell you, if that's how the world goes. He's arrested and in prison by now. They planned it all, the three of them."

"Quick, Josie, get dressed, and I will too. We must leave at once."

Josie may have been about to demur but Candy repeated desperately: "Josie, don't you understand!"

"Yes, Miss Candy, I understand," said Josie, and strangely enough she did. In fact, Josie had never felt so clear. It was almost as though now at last she had been given a taste of youth. Although it might come too late, it pierced her, nonetheless, and stifled her prudence. She did as she was told. Josie let her hand drop as though its weight were too great to be sustained. She had carried her back-stairs knowledge around with her too long and was probably glad enough now to let it go.

Candy started to dress. 'I must look older,' she thought to herself and pinned up the horsetail of hair to a flat bun on her head. This severe style suited the smooth oval of her face but brought out as well the Indian density of its secret lines. She took from her drawer a sample lipstick which she had purchased long ago at Woolworths when Josie had been in a lenient mood. The color was cheap and it made of her mouth a harsh smear without fullness or warmth, yet it was exciting, this crude smear across her face, a mark as if initiation or love. She reached into her shoebag and drew out from the toe of her country brogues the money given her by Giovanni. 'There,' she thought, standing still a minute to calm the turmoil, the lurching of her heart. 'There, I am as ready as ever I will be.'

A few minutes later, the servant and the young girl both left thc house.

It did not occur to Candy that Giovanni had been arrested outside. She thought he had been taken directly from No. 7, as though her father had said: "Arrest that man. He has tampered with my daughter!" Therefore she knew exactly where she was going. On her walks with Josie she had passed a police station and she remembered where it was. It was the only one in the city as far as she was concerned, and, in the confidence of her simplicity, she was right. She walked in, Josie following, and asked quietly:

"Where is Giovanni Puchini?"

The policemen in the room stared at this strange couple and the officer behind the desk, who had been doing a crossword puzzle, took off his glasses. "Who is Giovanni Puchini?"

"He is your prisoner," said Candy.

The officer blinked at Josie and then seemed to consult a list behind the counter. "Giovanni Puchini," he read. "Yes, we got him. He'll be taken round to the Tombs in the morning. You can see him in the line-up."

"What did he do?" asked Candy.

The officer replaced his glasses. "Are you over twenty-one?" he asked. "It's against the regulations to tell you if you're not." Then, finishing his scrutiny, he concluded: "And you're not."

Candy did not press the point or even mention that he might tell Josie. "How do I get to the Tombs?" she asked.

"Subway." He did not seem to wish for a continuation of their conversation and turned back to his paper, but as Candy and Josie were leaving, one of the policemen who had been sitting on a bench, got up, spat, rubbed the spittle into the floor, and advised:

"Take a taxi."

The Tombs, when they arrived, turned out to be a group of immense, pale blocks, cold and heartless beneath the dawn. From the outside they gave no hint of life within and repelled all questions. Josie, who had hardly spoken until now, said: “Miss Candy, we are too early. We’ll have some coffee.”

They went into an all-night cafeteria. Now that she was here and knew that Giovanni would be here too, Candy was calm and they sat there until daylight, drinking coffee at a table by the window and saying nothing to one another. Candy watched the last stars pale in the sky and the big, late moon grow dim so that the street showed grey. Now the blazing, starry night was over and the usual tawdry city morning took its place. Josie, too, looked out the window and up at the sky. Her thick glasses could not hide the tiredness of her eyes, which were red-rimmed and raw. Her forehead was perplexed with its usual wrinkles, while the deep lines between nostrils and mouth expressed her habitual cares. It was impossible to tell whether or not she regretted doing as Candy wished.

Around them sailors who had to get back to ships rubbed their eyes desperately as they drank black coffee and rehearsed the past evening with other Jacks. Sliding their faces around at Candy, they made their stories better. Nonetheless, one could see they were disillusioned. It had been, after all, no better than other times.

Big fat Irishwomen who swept out offices formed their own clan. Their loud laughter, their jokes, filled the air for about twenty minutes. Then they left and took buses uptown wherein they would torment the driver with their coarse, Celtic tongues. Early whitecollar workers walked in with red noses and pale cheeks. The women looked strained in their attempts to be smart. They were marvelously well kept, as though coated top to toe in lacquer. It gave them a sort of pathos which took the place of attraction. They could hardly be told apart from the prostitutes who were sitting demurely, two and two, refreshing themselves after work.

Candy saw none of these people and when she judged it late enough she got up. "Come, Josie, we must go and inquire."

There was no difficulty. Everybody knew all about the line-up. It was a sort of show or theatrical performance and the pair took their seats as among an audience. When Giovanni was brought in with his bruised eye and his shamefaced walk, Candy could hardly recognize him. But when, after he had been charged, he looked up and their glances met, she felt as though a strong light had been switched on somewhere in the middle of her body. It was as if a brightness had been held up for an instant against the rhythm and flow of her existence. And this sudden light was as painful as a torch flashed into the eyes at night. Candy gave a little gasp and left the room so fast that Josie did not know she had gone until she had disappeared.

Someone noted Candy, however. She had not got to the stairs when she felt a hand on her arm and turned to see a dark, middle-aged man with glasses and a shiny nose.

"Miss, can I help you?" He thrust a card in her face, from which she gathered he was Mr. Bower, an attorney. He withdrew the card and put it back in his wallet. "Got someone in there?" he asked, jerking his thumb towards the room she had quitted.

"Yes, and I want to bail him out."

"You got money?" Mr. Bower's voice sounded offhand.

"Yes," said Candy, "lots."

"Just you come to my office," said Mr. Bower, "and I'll fix you up. You have the money with you?"

"Yes," said Candy.

Mr. Bower's office was small and Candy spent a long time there. Mr. Bower himself came and went. Giovanni's bail was high, said Mr. Bower, and he was better off where he was. He, Mr. Bower, was going into the case and it was a serious charge. No, of course it wasn't true, but these things were difficult. Five hundred dollars was all she had? He had understood—Well, he would do his best. It was a difficult case. *In flagrante*—Where could he contact her?

"You can't," said Candy. "I must hire you today and you must do your best. Have you seen him?"

"Yes," said Mr. Bower, giving her a strange look full of disrespect. "I've seen him."

Candy caught the look and met it so that he saw into her eyes and into their shallow, incorruptible clarity. For an instant, Mr. Bower was puzzled. What *was* the setup?

"I'll do my best for you," he said with almost an honest ring in his voice.

Candy rose to go. She put the money down on the desk as if it were nothing. "And will you give him this, please?" She put an envelope into his hand, gave a slight nod or bow, and left. She was tired and it was already afternoon. Hailing a taxi, she rode home leaning back in the cab with closed eyes. She rang her doorbell and said to Harris when he came:

"Pay the taxi, please, and tell Father that I am here."

There was no need, as it turned out, for Charles to be told. He came running down the stairs and took his daughter's hands and embraced her warmly.

"Candy, *cherie!* I knew you would come back. Josie appeared here an hour ago and she was like a crazy woman, but *I* remained calm. I do not blame her, poor woman, she had no finesse. She cannot feel things as I do—as *we* do! Now you must take your place in this house, among my guests, and I will tell them to remove those dreadful bands from your teeth. Also I will buy you a beautiful lipstick, just the right shade for your skin!"

21

THE DUKE WAS FEELING benevolent. Late spring was in full glory. He had risen in good spirits and it was a lovely day. Also he had found a manager who was anxious, with the proper backing, to handle his puppet show. Charles stepped briskly out of his room and went into his study where the secretary was at work as usual.

Nigel and Pere Laborde came in together at that moment, as though summoned by the telepathy of their patron's good humor. Nigel was looking smooth and sleek. The charlatan Neju had been definitely replaced by the successful dilettante Nigel who made those witty, cruel dolls. And if those dolls had once contained a far more sinister power, well, one couldn't have everything. Pere Laborde, on the contrary, did not look well. He had an air of wishing to curry favor and of knowing it to be useless in advance. He had received another letter from his order and had a terrible certainty that, were he defrocked, Charles would be the first to hold up his hands in pious horror. And the course of returning to a monastic life grew more unthinkable with each succeeding day.

"Ah," said Charles, looking out the window, "how pure the air is now that those imbeciles have put the street together again." His beard marked his thin jaws, his eyelid twitched. He smiled. "Now, my friend," he said to the secretary, "I shall dictate a letter." The secretary took up his pencil.

"My dear Giovanni," the Duke began, placing himself in an attitude with his hand on the edge of the desk:

My dear Giovanni:

I once thought of you as a son and, although I realize now that this was a foolish, an impossible dream, I still have for you, in your sad plight, a paternal sorrow. There are three years ahead of you in which you must expiate your folly and wrongdoing. I hope that they will not make you bitter or hard; that they will, on the contrary, serve to show you the true path to a useful life.

You have erred, Giovanni, and three years is a small sentence compared to the penalty of many another. Yet I feel there is enough strength and essential goodness in your soul to overcome this unfortunate start.

When at last you emerge, purged and cleansed of your guilt, I will be, as now,

Your well-wisher—

"It is beautiful!" cried the priest when Charles had finished dictating. Pere Laborde really seemed to believe himself. Nigel gave him a curious and contemptuous glance and said to Charles:

"That will make him reflect!"

The Duke frowned.

Then they noticed that Candy had come in and was standing near. Nigel tactfully left the room. The priest, fluttering at the doorway an instant, finally left too. The secretary, who was doing his usual half-stand, half-sit, tried to look as though he were doing neither.

"Good morning, *cherie!*" Charles greeted her enthusiastically. "What do you think of my letter? I want to sound just, but hopeful. Is it all right? You know, of course, that they have given him three years?"

"No, I did not know, Papa," said Candy.

Her father looked at her face in silence, then took her hand gaily. *"Cherie,"* he said, "it has been decided that you come with us when we go abroad. It's time you met some of the nobility of Europe, and your mother agrees."

"Does she really, Papa? I thought she wanted me to meet no one until I was eighteen."

"Cherie, your mother is such a strange woman," cried Charles with a look of dismay.

Candy left the room soon after and went her ways and kept her thoughts to herself. The pale spring moon, coming in her window that night, shone on her so limpidly that her eyes seemed filled with tears. Yet everyone knew that Candy never wept.

Now Giovanni, lying with open eyes on his prison cot, had a dream, a waking dream, an imagining. He fancied that he was once again in his room in No. 7 and that Candy came through the door just as she once had. Only this time he did all the things that he had left undone before, those sublime things one does with a young girl who is in love, whom one loves. He took her by the hand and drew her gently to him. He caressed her shining head and kissed her long eyes and her mouth. He touched her pale cheeks and breathed in the warm, quick, uneven breath of her nostrils. Then he leaned upon her breast and held her so close against him, bone to bone, that he could feel her heart ache between his arms.

But Giovanni found that it was his own heart that was aching and he sat up on his cot and reached inside his shirt.

He took out from against his skin a lock of hair which the lawyer had given him in an envelope. He threw the long, slightly curving black lock away from him to the floor of the cell.

"My God!" he cried outloud: "Are women ever too young to be crazy?" and his voice broke with derision as he continued: "Does she think I'm going to spend the next three years necking with an old piece of dead grass?"

The End

CPSIA information can be obtained at www.ICGtesting.com
Printed in the USA
BVOW03s1205161013

333906BV00014B/525/P

9 781596 545663